**More praise for**
**THE SHERIFF AND**
**THE PANHANDLE MURDERS**

"The scene is in the mythical town of Carroll in a mythical Texas county, Crawford County. Meredith has truly caught the atmosphere of such places—the 'Texas' feeling and language. . . . Let's hope she continues."

*Houston Chronicle*

"It is one of the delights of Meredith's 'Sheriff' novels that she knows the Panhandle country and Panhandle people so well that she can mirror not only what it must be like to be a lawman there but what it *is* like to live there."

*El Paso Herald-Post*

"Very good . . . with some unusual twists . . . Even the seasoned reader should be cautious: this is a very cleverly thought-out novel."

*The El Paso Times*

# THE SHERIFF
# AND THE
# PANHANDLE
# MURDERS

## D. R. Meredith

BALLANTINE BOOKS • NEW YORK

Copyright © 1984 by D.R. Meredith

All rights reserved under International and Pan-American Copyright Conventions. Published in the United States of America by Ballantine Books, a division of Random House, Inc., New York, and simultaneously in Canada by Random House of Canada Limited, Toronto. Originally published by Walker Publishing Co., Inc. in 1984

All of the characters and events portrayed in this story are fictitious.

Library of Congress Catalog Card Number: 91-92105

ISBN 0-345-36951-3

Manufactured in the United States of America

First Edition: November 1991

To Nikki, who typed it,
And John, who let her,
And Mike, most of all:
My thanks

# ACKNOWLEDGMENTS

Buck Weaver and the Moore County Sheriff's Department
Jim Sadler and the Dumas Noon Lions Club
Stan Folsom
John Jowell

# CHAPTER

# 1

BILLY JOE WILLIAMS WAS SCARED, A BONE-DEEP KIND of scared that made him shift on the old pickup's worn upholstery as if he were sitting on a red-ant bed. He peered through the windshield at the newly risen sun as if it were wholly responsible for the acrid perspiration that made the pickup cab smell like a locker room at halftime and plastered his shirt to his skinny chest.

"Damn heat," he muttered. He swallowed and spat out the window in an unsuccessful attempt to rid himself of the sour taste of last night's beer. He wiped his sleeve across his mouth and spat again.

"Damn cheap beer! Ole Billy Joe is goin' to be drinkin' the best liquor from now on. No more of that rotgut crap."

He tapped his fingers on the steering wheel in time to the radio's raucous gospel music, lost in a recurring fantasy of fine whiskey and willing women. The fact that there had been a shortage of willing women in his life, and that the chances were good the shortage would continue, good liquor or not, didn't disturb him. Billy Joe made it a habit to ignore unpleasant facts. When the radio abruptly died with a final shrill, mechanical squeal, he pounded on the dashboard, disturbing the thick layer of Texas Panhandle dust.

"Damn radio! I gotta get a new pickup. Hell, yes, that's what I'm gonna do. I'm gonna go to the Ford place and git me a new pickup. It's gonna have one of them fancy murals on the back window and bright red vinyl seats."

Billy Joe swallowed again, thinking of bright, shining drops of blood splattering on the asphalt, blood the color of shiny red vinyl. "I think I'll git me a blue one instead; every wetback in town has got a red pickup."

He cleared this throat and glanced out the window at the eight-foot-tall rows of corn lining Farm to Market Road 1283. There was nothing to be seen he hadn't seen all his life. Desperately he continued his soliloquy to his new pickup. Even talking to himself was better than the silence.

"I'm gonna have me the best pickup in Crawford County. I'll get me one with air conditioning, stereo AM-FM radio, and a tape deck, and I'm gonna git a pair of handmade boots. I ain't never had a pair of handmade boots before. Can't drive a new pickup in these old things." He sneered at the cracked, mud-encrusted boots on his feet. "Billy Joe Williams, something's gonna turn out right for you. I'll be beating the girls off with a stick. I'll drive out to the rodeo arena and pick up one of them girls in the tight Levi's and I'll have me a hell of a time."

Unbidden, the vision of another kind of girl, a broken doll of a girl sprawled in the weeds on the side of the road, overshadowed his fantasy. Billy Joe felt the acrid bile rising in his throat again and swallowed desperately. His tongue flicked over the thin lips crowned by a scraggly blond mustache. The headlights of the pickup had seemed to focus on the girl, leaving the man's face cast in shadow. But he wasn't in the shadow enough; ole Billy Joe had recognized him right off.

"By damn, ole Billy Joe Williams is gonna have a brand-new pickup, or ole Billy Joe's gonna make a phone call to the county sheriff. That old S.O.B. don't like killin'; won't even let the Mexicans kill each other."

Billy Joe wrinkled his brow in his effort to analyze the sheriff. There was something about him that scared the hell out of a person. Something about the way he could look at you with those eyes of his made you want to walk easy around him. Billy Joe shrugged his shoulders; there was just no understanding the sheriff.

He peered through the windshield at the rapidly brightening early-morning sun, its red-orange color changing to blazing white.

"Damn sun! A man can't hardly see, drivin' straight at it

like this. Why the hell did he want to meet me clear out here?''

The rear wheel rolled over a rock, bouncing it up to hit the bed of the pickup with a dull thud.

"Sweet Jesus!" screamed Billy Joe as he pivoted his head around. Remembered sounds surrounded him: loud voices, the sound of a watermelon being smashed—only it wasn't a watermelon—the grunt of a man picking up a weight, the dull echo of boots on an asphalt road, the thud of a body being dropped into the bed of a pickup erupted from his memory. Images of long, black hair against a red-checked shirt, and blood running freely to finally splash on the asphalt, sank into his mind like irrigation water into thirsty Texas soil.

The front wheel slid off the asphalt onto the dirt shoulder, and Billy Joe fought the pickup back onto the road, only to slam on the brakes, lean out the window, and retch helplessly until he finally succeeded in emptying his stomach. Grimacing, he spat, hoping to cleanse his mouth of its foul taste. He rested his head against the steering wheel and breathed deeply. He ran his hands through his thin, blond hair and jerked upright to stare out the window at his Stetson hat, now stained with flecks of vomit.

He put his hand on the door handle, then hesitated. He felt safe inside the pickup; besides, he didn't want to be late. He didn't trust that S.O.B. to wait for him; he was awful snotty over the phone. He took one last look at his old Stetson and drove off, intent on his anger. "Damn bastard! You're gonna owe me a new hat!"

There was no reason why he should have heard the faint buzzing of an approaching spray plane. Spray planes at dawn were a common occurrence in the Texas Panhandle. Spraying was done only at dawn and dusk to avoid the ever-present wind.

Had he not been so preoccupied, he might have wondered why the plane was flying down the middle of the road instead of crisscrossing the fields on either side. It wouldn't have mattered, because there was nowhere for him to run. The release of the parathion from the plane's tanks and Billy Joe's muttered "Sweet Jesus!" came at the same time.

"No! No!" screamed Billy Joe as the acrid chemical filled

the cab of the pickup to sear his lungs and belly. He let go of
the steering wheel and grabbed his throat, clawing at the neck
of his shirt in a futile attempt to draw a breath of clean air. The
pickup veered off the road to roll into a deep bar ditch, coming
to rest upside down. Billy Joe was mindless of any outside
threat. Stunned by a blow to his head caused from hitting the
dashboard, Billy Joe was strangling on his own vomit.

The small yellow spray plane, its wings thick and swollen
with its now empty tanks, circled the pickup before landing on
the road. Its door opened, and a man climbed out. He stood by
the plane for a few minutes, watching the pickup with its
wheels still rotating as if reaching for a road no longer there.
He pulled a handkerchief out of his pocket and tied it around
his head to cover his nose and mouth. Walking to the bar ditch,
he squatted down to peer through the open window at Billy
Joe's unconscious form, his chest heaving in an involuntary
effort to clear the clotted breathing passages.

A daring man, but one who didn't take unnecessary risks, he
pinched Billy Joe's nostrils closed with one hand and held his
other over the gasping mouth. Patiently he waited, breathing
shallowly to try to avoid the heavy chemicals and occasionally
glancing at his watch. At the end of five minutes he rose to his
feet, grimacing at his vomit-smeared gloves. He pulled the
bandana off his face and stood, hands on hips, an impersonal
smile thinning the full lips. Then he raised his hand in a mocking salute and returned to the spray plane with a firm, unhur-
ried step.

# CHAPTER

# 2

SHERIFF CHARLES TIMOTHY MATTHEWS WAS BORN and reared in the urban sprawl of Dallas. Since most natives of Dallas and points south considered the Panhandle to be an area of ignorant cowboys and hick farmers whose drawls were thick enough to plant wheat in, his presence in Crawford County, Texas, was inexplicable to his family and friends.

His law degree didn't necessarily set Charles apart from others but his graduation from Rice University did. Kids from the Panhandle generally attended West Texas State, Texas Tech, or Texas A & M. Rice University is almost as exotic a school as Harvard, except that its graduates are more trusted; after all, Rice is in Houston.

But the single most distinctive aspect of Charles Timothy Matthews was his lack of a nickname. In the Panhandle, nicknames are as common as sagebrush, yucca plants, and grasshoppers. Charles Timothy Matthews was always addressed as "Charles." Persons calling him "Charlie" or "Chuck" were always politely but firmly corrected. He seldom had to correct anyone more than once. There was a certain aura about him that unconsciously impressed everyone that here was a man who meant what he said.

When asked, as he frequently was that first year, why he had chosen Carroll, county seat of Crawford County, as his new home, Charles would smile gently and reply that the town seemed to be a fine place to live. No one asked why he had left Dallas in the first place. Enough of the Old West philosophy lingered in Carroll to prevent their asking about his past; a man was still accepted at face value until proven otherwise.

Only his intimate friends knew the truth: Carroll was as far as he could drive from Dallas in one day and still stay in Texas.

"Actually, L.D.," Charles said, slumping deeper into the overstuffed couch, "Carroll had another advantage besides just being a day's drive from Dallas."

"What's that?" asked L.D. Lassiter, Crawford County attorney and hometown boy.

"Carroll had a liquor store at the edge of town, and I badly needed a drink at that particular time."

"Charles, if the town ever hears you say that, the citizens will tar you with liquid manure, roll you in tumbleweeds, and ride you out of town in a horse trailer," Angie Lassiter said as she appeared from the kitchen with a tray laden with cold cuts, beer, and crackers.

Charles grinned at her. "May I depend on you to keep my secret?"

Angie smiled as she set the tray down. "I think I'll just hold that information over your head, Charles, in case I need it to keep you in line. Enjoy yourselves, gentlemen; I'm going to take a nap while the kids are asleep."

Charles reached for a beer and admired Angie's slim legs as she walked out of the room. He felt his unusual self-recrimination for wanting his best friend's wife. He often wondered why he tortured himself by spending so much time at L.D.'s house. He would never allow himself to tell her how he felt, yet he couldn't bring himself to stop taking advantage of every opportunity to be around her. The ringing of the telephone interrupted his thoughts, and he unconsciously rose to answer it.

"If it's a divorce client, I'm not here," said L.D., making himself a towering sandwich. "I'm sick and damn tired of people calling me on Sunday to tell me about their marital problems."

"Don't you know a lawyer is a father confessor?" asked Charles.

"Don't tell me! I'm the one who has to listen to them complain about their spouses, and they always insist on telling me more than I want or need to hear. You'd be amazed—"

"Charles, it's for you," Angie interrupted.

"This is the sheriff," he said, his voice lacking the familiar drawl of the region. He leaned against the kitchen wall and crossed one ankle over the other. A frown line appeared between his eyebrows and he straightened up, his fine-featured face assuming its usual stern lines.

"Where did it happen? Okay, tell Meenie I'll be right out." He hung up the phone and turned to L.D., a puzzled expression replacing the frown.

"Some farmer just found Billy Joe Williams's body out on 1283. I need to call the J.P. and get out there. Come with me, L.D.; Meenie thinks there's something funny about this one."

"Meenie would see something criminal about the Second Coming," L.D. said, disgust in his voice. "Let me tell Angie where I'm going, and get some shoes on." He padded into the bedroom, and Charles could hear his deep voice and Angie's murmured responses. Again he felt a stab of jealousy. "Always want what you can't have, don't you, Charles boy?" he asked himself. He smiled at his own bitterness and, turning, dialed the justice of the peace.

"Sammy, this is Charles. I need a pronouncement from you. A farmer found Billy Joe Williams out on 1283. Looks like a car wreck." Charles cursed silently at the strident voice coming from the phone. "I know it's Sunday afternoon, Sammy, but no one is officially dead until you say so. I'll have a patrol car pick you up. Thanks, Sammy," he said, without waiting to hear any more excuses.

"Damn him," Charles said as they left the house. "Next election, I'm putting up my own candidate for J.P. That man is too lazy to scratch his own fleas."

"Good luck, Charles; as long as the bastard dismisses all his friends' traffic tickets, the office is his for life."

"Don't be too sure; he's never had me after him before." Charles's voice was expressionless, and all the more frightening because of it.

Charles and L.D. got into the beige patrol car with its star-shaped insignia on the door. The make of car varied from year to year, depending on which local dealer got the bid, but the color and insignia never changed. The hum of the air conditioning and the staccato sounds of the police band radio formed a familiar background for their conversation.

"I suppose you will be ladling the beef and beans at the barbecue tomorrow?"

"Of course; it's my service club that sponsors Frontier Days, after all. Besides, it's a good time to see everybody in the county."

"Anyone would think you are running for reelection this year." Charles grinned.

"Anyone with any sense starts running for reelection from the day he is sworn in," L.D. said. "You need to remember that, Charles."

"I had enough of political trade-offs and maneuvering in Dallas, L.D., and I found I wasn't very good at it."

"You're a politician; county sheriff is an elective office," L.D. objected.

"But I won't play politics to stay here," Charles snapped, annoyed with the conversation. L.D. had polished the art of small-town politics to a high gloss, but it was one of his friend's accomplishments that Charles didn't admire.

They left the city limits and the air shimmered with the afternoon heat. Fields of maize rippled like green ocean waves as the hot summer wind blew across them. Pivot irrigation systems sprayed water through their aerial pipes, covering over a hundred acres at a time, turning an arid land into some of the most valuable farm property in the world. Charles turned onto Farm Road 1283 and picked up speed. The road was a tunnel between the corn fields that covered hundreds of acres on either side.

"How do you suppose Billy Joe could wreck his pickup out here? There's nothing to hit, and usually the bar ditch isn't deep enough to roll a vehicle," L.D. remarked.

"I don't know, but Meenie thought something was a little odd," Charles answered. "And if Meenie thinks something is odd, then you can depend on it being true."

Red flashing lights and a small group of people signaled the site of the wreck. Charles parked the patrol car on the shoulder of the road and climbed out. A short, bowlegged man dressed in the Sheriff's Department uniform of beige, western-cut pants and shirt detached himself from a small crowd of similarly dressed men that surrounded the battered pickup. Shifting a wad of tobacco from one cheek to the other, the man spat into the bar ditch, hitched up the trousers that threatened to slip off his skinny hips, and walked up to Charles.

"Sheriff, L.D." Meenie Higgins nodded at each man, rocking back and forth in his boots, thumbs hooked over his belt. "It's a funny one; looks like someone dumped a load of parathion right over his pickup."

"I didn't think spray pilots sprayed insecticides across roads. Was it an accident?" asked Charles, his long legs carrying him down the bar ditch to the pickup.

Meenie spat a stream of tobacco juice onto the asphalt. "If it was, no one reported it. Besides, there's traces of parathion for a hundred yards down the road. Don't generally fly down the middle of the highway sprayin' the stuff. Not too many grasshoppers on asphalt."

"Just a minute, Meenie," L.D. said. "Parathion can't kill anyone instantly, unless you held his head down in a tank of the stuff so he would drown."

"L.D.'s right; that chemical won't kill you, least ways not right away. But it sure as hell made him sick," Meenie said. "Looks like he hit his head on the dashboard, too."

Charles squinted through the window at the limp body, noting the vomit-flecked shirt. He looked around the cab of the pickup and finally asked, "Where's his hat?"

Meenie pushed his own hat to the back of his head, shifted his wad to the other cheek, and accurately struck a grasshopper with a stream of tobacco juice. "Don't know, Sheriff. Never saw old Billy Joe without his hat. Got to be around here somewhere?"

"Send someone down the road to see if it can be found. There's evidence on the side of the door that Billy Joe was sick more than once. Maybe he leaned out the window and his hat fell off." Charles rose and dusted off his trousers.

"What's so important about his hat, Charles?" L.D. asked as the two men moved away from the pickup to seek air less pungent with the smell of death and parathion.

"Billy Joe would never drive off and leave his hat. That

was a good Stetson he wore, and he couldn't afford another
one. No matter how sick he was, even if he had been sick
right on top of it, he would never have left it behind."
Charles shaded his eyes under his own broad-brimmed hat
and looked down the road that seemed to undulate in the oppressive heat.

"Let's talk to that farmer who discovered the wreck. Maybe
he noticed something." Charles walked over to a heavy-set
man in his middle thirties.

"I'm Sheriff Matthews," Charles said, shaking the man's
hand. "When did you discover the wreck?"

"Joe Davis, Sheriff," replied the man. "I was on my way
down to my corn field to check the irrigation water. Corn takes
a hell of a lot of water. I don't think I'm going to make a dime
on that crop, either; it hasn't rained in six weeks, and I've got
to irrigate every damn day. My hired hand quit last week, and
I've been meeting myself coming and going, just trying to stay
even with all the work."

"I'm sure it's difficult," Charles broke in smoothly. He had
lived in the Panhandle long enough to learn that a farmer could
spend hours discussing the price of irrigation gas, the rising
cost of seed, fertilizer, herbicide, and the ridiculously low
prices their crops brought in the marketplace. Charles was
sympathetic to the family farmer caught in the cost squeeze,
but he just didn't have time to listen today.

"Mr. Davis, if you would just give me a quick description
of what you found," Charles said.

"Well, I found just what you see. The pickup was upside
down in the ditch. I looked in and saw Billy Joe. I knew right
off he was dead. His eyes were open and glazed over. I got
back in my pickup and drove down to the house and called
your office. I didn't see nobody at all."

"What time was this, Mr. Davis?" Charles asked.

"About thirty minutes ago," replied the farmer, checking
his watch. "Must have been about three o'clock or so."

"Okay, thank you. Go on back to town with my deputy Raul
Trujillo and give him a statement."

"Do you mind if I go check my irrigation water first, Sheriff? God knows, I should have done it earlier, but the wife's folks came to dinner, and I was late getting started.''

"Go ahead, Mr. Davis. Just drop by the office after you finish. And thank you again.'' Charles watched the man hurry over to his pickup and drive off.

The sound of a siren and flashing lights signaled the approach of another patrol car. It screeched to a halt and an enormous man with a matching belly unfolded himself from the front seat. A well-chewed cigar was clamped between his teeth, and a network of tiny veins on his nose and cheeks indicated an excessive fondness for fermented beverages. He took his cigar out of his mouth and picked flecks of tobacco off the protruding lower lip.

"All right, Sheriff, where is this body I have to look at?'' Sammy Phillips's voice managed to combine a strident quality with a nasal tone, a combination that immediately set Charles's teeth on edge.

"Right over here. And Sammy, I want an autopsy ordered.'' Charles's voice and face were expressionless, but their very lack of expression lent him an uncompromising authority.

''Now wait jest a minute, Sheriff. I'm the one who makes that decision. Ain't no sense in spending the county's money for an autopsy on a car wreck victim. Some of you elected officials are always spendin' money like it was water, but not Sammy Phillips, no sir. There ain't gonna be no autopsy when it ain't necessary.'' Sammy panted with exertion as he climbed down the steep bank of the bar ditch to peer in the window at Billy Joe's body.

"Sammy!'' Charles's voice cracked like breaking glass. "There is no visible injury to Billy Joe that could be fatal. When that is the case, the law requires an autopsy to determine the exact cause of death.'' Charles waited a moment as he and the J.P. exchanged glances, two adversaries preparing for a duel. "I'm sure you don't want the good citizens of Crawford County believing that you are incapable of performing the duties of your office.''

Sammy laboriously pulled himself to his feet and stood in front of the sheriff, a whine now becoming evident in his voice. "Now, Sheriff, I told you that I didn't like ordering autopsies for every Tom, Dick, and Harry that gets drunk and piles up his pickup in a bar ditch.''

Charles inspected his nails for a moment, then looked at Sammy, a bland expression on his face. "I got an interesting report by teletype the other day, Sammy. It had to do with one of our local citizens, one of our prominent local citizens, being drunk and disorderly in a public bar downstate. You wouldn't know who that prominent citizen was, would you, Sammy?'' Charles held up his hand as the J.P.'s face reddened and he seemed ready to explode. "Another interesting thing about that report, Sammy, was the information that the companion of said local citizen was remanded to juvenile court.'' Charles's voice lowered to a whisper threaded with disgust. "That means the companion was under seventeen, Sammy.''

The J.P. pulled a handkerchief out of his pocket and wiped his face, then carefully ran it around the inside lining of his straw Stetson. He cleared his throat noisily and blew his nose with the same sweat-stained handkerchief. He licked his fleshy lower lip and replaced his hat, setting it squarely on his head. He looked at the cigar held between his fingers as though wondering how it came to be there.

"It seems to me, Sheriff, that the death of that poor boy over there needs further investigation. I'm going to order an autopsy just to satisfy myself.'' Sammy wiped his face again and climbed back in the patrol car. "Hey, you," he yelled out to one of the deputies, "drive me home." He glared at Charles momentarily, but his eyes shifted away from direct contact with the chilling brown ones of the sheriff.

Charles watched the patrol car reverse direction and head back to town. He didn't regret his tactics with Sammy at all. If his stint in the Dallas district attorney's office had taught him nothing else, it had taught him to fight politicians on their own terms.

"Raul," Charles motioned to a olive-skinned deputy standing motionless by the side of the road, "get some pictures of the pickup and the body.'' Raul nodded silently and went to get the field camera from his car. Charles turned as Meenie stepped to his side, holding a Stetson.

"This is it, Sheriff. Found it about a quarter mile down

the road. Must have fell off his head when he got sick, and he just drove off and left it. Found some skid marks in the dirt by the side of the road a little farther back. Billy Joe sure wasn't paying much attention to his drivin'." Meenie shifted his tobacco again and turned his head to spit.

"That's kind of strange, too, Sheriff. Ole Billy Joe was a good driver. He never had a ticket in his life; used to brag about it. I guess it was the only thing he ever had to brag about. He wasn't good for much, but he sure could drive."

Charles shifted uncomfortably, feeling the hot sun burning through his sports shirt. He felt the need of some cold beer to wash the dry Panhandle dust out of his mouth. He smiled bitterly to himself. It wasn't the dust that was drying out his mouth and throat, but the familiar fury he always felt in the presence of death, particularly violent, unnecessary death.

"Meenie, you and Raul find out everything you can about Billy Joe. I especially want to know where he was last night and whom he talked to. I want know what he was doing here. Was he driving to work?"

"Hell, Sheriff, Billy Joe couldn't hold down a job for more than a month at a time. No farmer in his right mind would let him around any machinery; he was too damn careless. None of the ranchers would hire him as a cowboy 'cause he couldn't stay on a horse. Whatever he was doing out here, it sure wasn't drivin' to work." Meenie shifted his tobacco again and spat, striking a beetle crawling along the road.

"Crying shame, Sheriff; Billy Joe never did no harm to anyone. He was kind of a useless human being, but he wasn't bad." Meenie rubbed the stubble on his jaw thoughtfully. He was always trying to cultivate a beard, and would let his whiskers grow until his chin looked like a scraggly pincushion. "What do you think happened, Sheriff?"

"He doesn't appear to be seriously injured from the wreck, and you natives assure me parathion wouldn't kill him." Charles shrugged his shoulders. "I'd say that leaves the case wide open."

Abruptly he turned his back to the wrecked pickup and its pitiful occupant. "Tell the mortician to take the body to Amarillo for an autopsy, and find out who was spraying parathion this morning.''

"Hell, that could be half of the county, Sheriff; everybody's trying to keep the grasshoppers out of their crops.''

"Then we'll just question half the county if that's what it takes. Billy Joe Williams might have been shiftless, but he was still worth more than a grasshopper.''

# CHAPTER

# 3

AS THE MONDAY MORNING SUN WAS REFLECTING off the shattered windshield of Billy Joe Williams's pickup, the town of Carroll, or at least many of its male members, were donning dark glasses against its glare. Businessmen and farmers, ranchers and professionals began arriving in a steady stream at a local pasture. They gathered in small groups, exchanging gossip and cursing the rising temperature.

Forming a background to the crowd was the reason for its assembling: a three-hundred-foot trench, four feet deep and four feet wide. Covered over with sheet metal, then dirt, the pit contained the coals of fifteen cords of mesquite layered over with more than three tons of beef. The Frontier Days Barbecue, enough to feed over seven thousand people, was ready to be uncovered, loaded onto pickups, driven to the country courthouse lawn, and served to all comers.

A tall, sturdy figure, his white cowboy shirt bearing his name stitched in red above the pocket, wove in and out of the crowd.

"Curly, you got your pickup ready? You're taking the first load to town." His voice was loud and brassy, a perfect carnival barker.

"Sure thing, Jim Bob; got it parked right at the end of the trench," answered a thin, wiry man, nervously pushing up his wire-rimmed glasses.

Jim Bob Brown clapped the grocer on the back, sending his glasses back down his thin nose. "Good man! I knew I could count on you to follow orders." Jim Bob rubbed his hands together enthusiastically. "Leon, are you ready with the front end loader?"

15

A tall, trim man in his middle forties waved his arm. "Ready, Jim Bob."

Jim Bob stood a moment, his hands lifted melodramatically. One year a practical joker had given him two checkered flags similar to those used at car races. He had not been amused. "This is not some silly game, you idiot; this is serious!" he had roared, and broken the flags over his knee. There were those who said Jim Bob enjoyed giving the signal to uncover the barbecue pit more than he enjoyed being a county commissioner; certainly he was more efficient at it. Jim Bob had a tendency to fall asleep at commission meetings.

"Go to it, Leon!" shouted Jim Bob, bringing his arms down.

The front end loader slowly moved forward to begin scooping the mound of dirt off the sheet metal. Forward, then backward, Leon methodically uncovered the pit. Several men in identical white shirts ran forward to pull off the sheet metal. Others began grabbing burlap sacks filled with meat and heaving them up into waiting hands, to be stacked in Curly's pickup. As it was filled, another took its place. The entire process normally took no more than an hour.

L.D. observed Jim Bob's posturing while finishing off a cold beer. He watched the milling crowd of men and wondered how these dissimilar personalities always managed to pull themselves together to put on what was one of the biggest and one of the best outdoor barbecues in the world. Sighing, he contemplated drinking another beer, but decided he'd better wait. Putting on the heavy cotton gloves habitually worn by all club members on Barbecue Day, he took his place in line by the edge of the pit.

One pickup pulled away loaded with the spicy, succulent beef, while still another took its place. The front end loader was now more than halfway down the three-hundred-foot trench, with the men right behind it. Sweat was beginning to bead on foreheads as the sun climbed higher. Doggedly, they continued down the trench toward the far end.

As the next to the last piece of sheet metal was uncovered, the crowd fell silent. A faint odor that had nagged at many of them was becoming stronger. Jim Bob's voice was unnaturally loud in the hushed air.

"What the devil is that smell?"

Jim Bob plowed through the unresisting bodies, a bulldozer of a man, his eyes intent on his goal. L.D. caught his belt to halt his forward progress.

"I'll go with you," he said as a gust of the Panhandle's generous daily allowance of wind brought a stronger whiff of the stench emanating from the pit. The malevolent odor caught Jim Bob, almost doubling him over, and his protest at L.D.'s presumptuousness died.

"I'd appreciate it, L.D." Reluctantly, instinct slowing their steps, they approached the pit. Catching the sheet metal at each end, they pulled it off. The other men stood waiting, the silence building tension to an unbearable peak. Jim Bob and L.D. grabbed the sacks of meat, heaving them out of the pit onto the ground. L.D. worked in grim silence while Jim Bob gave voice to a steady stream of curses.

"Oh my God!" he screamed, tottering backward away from the pit, holding the burlap sack of meat like a shield. His mouth opened and closed, then the sack was dropped as he fell to his knees, retching helplessly.

L.D. recoiled from the pit, the image of a half-burned body lingering on his retina. He grabbed the arm of the nearest man. "Go get the sheriff," he ordered hoarsely; "tell him there's a body in the barbecue pit."

# CHAPTER

# 4

CHARLES STARED AT THE TWO FILES ON HIS DESK. They contained the preliminary reports on the victim in the barbecue pit and on Billy Joe Williams. He opened the folder on Billy Joe and read Meenie's poorly typed report. He tapped his fingers on his desk. Dammit, he had to know what happened to Billy Joe. He had to clear his mind of one death before he could take on another. He wanted to be able to dismiss Billy Joe as an accidental death. He wanted his intuitive unease to be wrong—just another example of his habit of looking for patterns in events. Some things were coincidental; let this be one of them.

Dialing a number, Charles propped his feet on his desk and settled back in his chair.

"Hello, this is Sheriff Matthews from Carroll. I want to talk to Dr. Akin. No, I'll wait; just tell him who's calling." Charles leaned his head back and gazed at the tall ceiling with its old, wooden-bladed fan. A loud voice jerked his attention back to the phone.

"Sheriff, this is Dr. Akin. You're pushing, Charles; I haven't had time to get much done on this latest body. What's happening up there anyway? I don't get an autopsy a year out of Crawford County; all of a sudden, I get two in two days. You people having a crime wave? Your homicide rate per capita is higher than Houston's." Dr. Akin's voice was testy; he was used to working with people who didn't talk back.

Charles closed his eyes. Homicide! His intuition was right. Crawford County hadn't had a deliberate well-planned, cold-blooded murder in over eight years and all of a sudden it has two. "I see you haven't lost your sense of humor, Doctor, but we up here are not finding anything to laugh at. Now tell me about Billy Joe Williams.''

"White, about twenty-five, just under six feet, basically in poor physical condition.''

"I know that, Doctor,'' said Charles, irritation beginning to creep into his voice. "What I need to know is the cause of death. Was it the parathion?''

"Sorry, Sheriff; I don't mean to make fun at your expense. In a word, no, parathion did not kill him. It would have made him mighty sick if he had lived, possibly shortened his life span, but it did not kill him. Billy Joe Williams suffocated to death.''

"You mean someone strangled him?'' asked Charles.

"I mean that in my expert opinion someone suffocated him. He was aspirating his own vomit, but under normal conditions, involuntary coughing should have cleared the air passages. Indeed, judging from the amount of vomit found in his mouth, this was occurring. However, the substances never left the mouth.''

"Why not?'' asked Charles.

"If one's mouth is held closed, then it is very difficult to spit something out,'' replied the doctor. Dr. Akin was the only person who could make Charles feel like an idiot.

"Is there proof of that?''

"Unfortunately not. But there are the blue marks, bruises, on either side of the nostrils as if someone had pinched them shut. Fortunately this young man bruised easily. Also there are ruptured blood vessels in the eyes that are a dead giveaway. You always find them in a suffocation or strangulation.''

"What about the other body, Doctor? Can you give me any information on it?''

"Other than it was female, between the ages of sixteen and eighteen, had perfect teeth, and had suffered a compound fracture of the left tibia as a youngster, I can't tell you much about her. There is a severe head injury of very recent origin, but I don't know if that was the cause of death. I am not a miracle worker, Sheriff; autopsies take time. However, if you keep sending me bodies on a daily basis, I do plan to hire another assistant or two.''

"Don't hire them on my account, Doctor; I hope the crime wave is over," Charles said trimly. "Thanks, and call me immediately on the girl's body; I don't care what time it is."

Charles hung up the phone and picked up the pile of statements taken by Raul. He read Jim Bob Brown's and whistled soundlessly. The pit had been dug a day early this year, and from late Saturday until Sunday morning had been open and filled with three and a half feet of mesquite wood. The body had to have been buried during that time because on Sunday morning at six, the mesquite was doused with the diesel fuel and set on fire. After a few hours to allow the wood to burn down, the meat was added and the whole thing was bulldozed over with dirt. The question was: who knew about the change of schedule?

Quickly Charles read the rest of the statements and sorted those who had known from those who hadn't. Rapidly he counted the two piles. Twenty-three men knew the pit was dug on Saturday. He reread the twenty-three statements and sorted them again. Ten of the twenty-three had no alibis for Saturday night, or at least none that would stand up under close scrutiny. Rising to his feet, he crossed to the door and jerked it open.

"Raul, get in here. I've got something for you." Without waiting for an affirmative response from the deputy, Charles walked back to his desk. Sitting down, he leaned back in his chair and put his feet on top of his desk.

"I wish I had my camera. You look like everybody's idea of a West Texas sheriff." Raul seemed amused.

Charles raised an eyebrow. "You know, that's one of the things I like about being a Panhandle sheriff. I can sit with my feet on my desk when I damn well feel like it."

"You're accepted, Sheriff; you are willing to take advice from the natives."

"You being one of the natives, I suppose?" asked Charles with a grin.

Raul smiled self-consciously and spread his hands in an eloquent Latin gesture. "No, I'm not. I'm still considered a Mexican."

Charles snorted in disgust. "Well, it's damn ridiculous. Now let's get back to basics. Write down these names and take a run out to the airport and find out how many of them are pilots. Then find out which ones were spraying yesterday.''

Charles slid the pile of papers across the desk to Raul. ''I called the coroner. Billy Joe Williams was murdered, and whoever killed him can pilot a spray plane. And whoever put the girl's body in the barbecue pit is a participant in the Frontier Days planning. I think it's unlikely we'd have two murders so close together and not have them related.''

Raul pulled out a small notebook and began to write down the names. ''You think the guilty one is among these men?''

''I think there is a good chance of it. The problem is motive. Damn it, Raul, we're working blind without a motive. We're not a sophisticated big city with a crime lab. We've got a fingerprint kit and a camera, and several hundred square miles in our jurisdiction, a lot of it uninhabited. The nearest pathologist is a hundred miles away. Our only hope of catching a murderer is first: motive, and second: character. We figure out why the victim is killed, and then study the characters of the suspects. And if—and it's a big if—if we're lucky, we can match the character to the motive and have our killer.''

''That's a lot of ifs.''

''I haven't mentioned the biggest if of all,'' said Charles bleakly. ''Even when logic and instinct tells us who the killer is, we still have to tie him to the crime with physical evidence. The only thing we have going for us is the fact that blood is damn hard to wash away. That body had to be taken to the pit in some kind of vehicle. If we can find the vehicle, we will be a long ways down the road to a conviction. Get going, Raul; I want some answers tonight.'' Charles dismissed his deputy with a wave of his hand and massaged the back of his neck. He stood up and walked over to the window and gazed down at the lawns around the courthouse.

Surrounded by elm trees, the red brick, three-story building stood in the middle of one square block in the center of Carroll. Every year during the first week of August the courthouse lawn and three of the four streets around it became a carnival ground. Rides and booths covered the lawn and spilled over into the streets. The crowd seemed quieter this year, less rowdy; word of the body had cast a pall over the usual high spirits. Small knots of people gathered under the tall elms. There was almost a furtive, suspicious air about the crowd, as if everyone not directly related was suspect.

Charles sighed and returned to his desk. Murders were always worse in a small town, because you usually knew both the victim and the guilty party. Suspicion of outsiders would run rampant, and since an outsider was defined as anyone who had lived in Crawford County less than thirty years, a lot of good people would be the subject of gossip.

Gradually he became aware of raised voices outside his door. He sighed and walked over to pull it open. The entire Mexican community of Carroll seemed to be filling the waiting room and spilling out into the hall. A man in his early thirties was the spokesman for the group. He effortlessly switched from English to Spanish as he translated a deputy's questions for a much older couple. Several other people, some of them women with small children, watched the proceedings with blank expressions.

"Roberto, what's the problem?" Charles asked, striding through the crowd to shake the young man's hand.

"Sheriff, I'm glad to see you." Roberto Martinez gestured at the crowd behind him. "Sorry to bring the whole family, but you know how it is."

Charles did indeed know how it is. Any meetings with officialdom, whether the police or a visit to the doctor, was a family occasion. Perhaps it was a defensive gesture of the Mexican minority when braving the halls of the Anglo majority.

"Is someone in your family in trouble, Roberto?"

"Maria, my youngest sister, is missing. The whole family has been searching the last two days. My father didn't want to go to the police, but I persuaded him. His English is not the best, and it embarrasses him to admit it. So I and my brothers and sisters agreed to come with him."

Charles listened, but heard nothing past the information about the missing girl. He hoped the sick dread he felt was not apparent.

"Roberto, would you and your parents come into my office, please?" He held the door open while Roberto herded his parents through. Charles closed the door and leaned against it for a moment, mentally preparing himself. God, how he wished someone else were doing it. Drawing a deep breath, he straightened and walked to his desk to sit on the edge of it.

"Roberto, how old is your sister?"

"She is seventeen, Sheriff. The smartest of all of us. She is the baby, and we spoil her a lot. But she is a good girl, not wild like some."

"Did Maria break her leg when she was younger?" Charles held his breath, hoping for a negative answer.

"Yes, she did; she broke her left leg when she was eight. Why do you ask?" Roberto had stiffened at the question.

"Did you take her to a local doctor, and did he take X-rays?" Charles felt sick; he wanted to know who the victim was, but he wasn't prepared for it to be the sister of a man he knew.

"Yes, we took her to a local doctor, and yes, he took X-rays. You know something about Maria, don't you, Sheriff?" Roberto's eyes were guarded as he built up defenses against the answer.

"Roberto, I can't be positive until the doctor has a chance to see those X-rays. The body we found this morning was about your sister's age, and she had had a broken left leg."

"Let me see her; I'll know if it's Maria." Roberto's voice broke.

"Roberto, haven't you heard about the body we discovered this morning?" Charles asked, desperately hoping to avoid having to tell him.

"No! What's wrong? What happened to Maria?" Roberto's eyes were fixed on Charles's face.

"Oh, my God," Charles said. "I thought everybody in the county knew by now." He took a deep breath, wishing Raul were there to help him. "The body was burned, Roberto, that's why we need the X-rays. There is no way to identify it otherwise."

"How was it burned, Sheriff? Was Maria in a car wreck?"

Charles wiped his hands over his face, wishing there were some euphemistic way to tell him. "The body was discovered in the barbecue pit."

"*Madre de Dios!*" The blood drained from Roberto's face

as the full horror hit him, leaving his olive complexion almost gray.

"We can't be positive, Roberto, but I didn't want to send you away with a lie, or without preparing you for the worst. The timing is right, the age is right, and there's a broken leg. It would be a miracle if it wasn't Maria's body." Charles dug his fingers through his hair. "My God! I'm sorry!"

Roberto's mother frantically tugged on her son's sleeve, fear making the lines on her face appear deeper. Roberto translated Charles's words, his voice trembling with his own unshed tears. Shock, then disbelief, scored her face. A keening sound came from somewhere deep in her throat, and she folded her arms across her breast as if she were holding a baby.

Charles felt empty and useless. He had no words to say that would comfort these people. He knelt beside the mother and stroked her hair and cursed his own helplessness, wondering if there had been another way to tell them, a kinder way. He blamed himself for his part in their grief, even as he prepared to question them.

"Roberto," he said softly, "I must ask questions. I must know everyone Maria knew. I have to have your answers before I can catch the murderer."

"I will kill him!" Roberto stated flatly.

"If you do, Roberto, I'll have to come after you."

"You will not find me."

"Then the murderer will have destroyed two lives instead of one."

"What if he's an Anglo, Sheriff? What will the state do then? Will it exact justice? Who cares about a Mexican girl from a poor family?"

"I care, Roberto. I care."

# CHAPTER

# 5

CHARLES GRIMACED AND SET HIS COFFEE CUP DOWN. The Crawford County Sheriff's Department had to have the worst coffee in the world. He once jokingly proposed to the county commissioners during a budget meeting that it be substituted for lye soap and used to clean the jail cells.

"Slim!" he yelled, and tapped his fingers impatiently on his desk until the lanky deputy appeared. "Can anyone around here make a pot of coffee without using half the can?"

Slim Fletcher scratched his head, clearly perplexed by the question. "I don't rightly know, Sheriff. I think everybody likes it pretty strong."

"Well, I don't. Make another pot and use a lighter hand with the coffee grounds. Is Meenie back yet?"

"Not yet, Sheriff," the deputy answered.

"Send him in as soon as he sticks his nose in the courthouse. And bring me a cup of coffee, a fresh cup of coffee."

"Sure thing, Sheriff." Slim retreated rapidly through the door.

Charles leaned back in his chair. He felt drained from the encounter with Roberto and his family. He'd have to go out there tomorrow and ask questions about Maria. He pulled a pad and pencil over and began jotting down notes.

For a moment he yearned for his job in the district attorney's office in Dallas. He had never known the victims there. They were just faceless beings whose identity did not touch his own life.

His thoughts were interrupted by Meenie's unceremonious entrance. Charles automatically hooked a toe around his spitoon and pushed it toward the chair at the corner of his desk.

Meenie shifted his wad and let fly with a stream of tobacco juice. Charles closed his eyes momentarily, knowing the law of averages dictated that Meenie had to miss that spitoon someday, and wondered if today were the day.

"You can open your eyes, Sheriff; I didn't miss."

"Did you find anything that might help?"

"Yeah, I found some metal eyelets that look to me like they came from a tarp. Other than that, there was a metal buckle, a little bit of a belt, and that's about it. Nothing that would really help. Tarps are a dime a dozen around here. The metal buckle and the belt were probably the victim's. Gonna be hard to tie anyone to this murder."

"The victim was most probably Maria Martinez."

"Maria! Roberto's baby sister? How do you know for sure?"

"I can't be certain, but Roberto was here with the whole family to report her missing. The time frame is right, the age is right, and the broken left leg is right. I had the X-rays sent on to Dr. Akin. It's ninety-nine percent sure it's Maria."

"That's too bad. The family thought a lot of that little girl and turned a blind eye to anything she did."

"What did she ever do? I've never heard anything about the girl," Charles said.

"She was ambitious, that little girl; she held herself out as being a little bit better than the rest of her people. Kind of pitiful, really. Her family is hardworking and honest; she should've been proud of them, instead of ashamed."

"There's nothing wrong with ambition, Meenie, and being embarrassed about one family's is something you outgrow."

"She'll never get a chance to do that, will she?" Meenie asked.

"No," Charles agreed, "she won't. Billy Joe Williams was murdered," he added abruptly.

"Coroner finally call?" asked Meenie.

"No, I called him. I was hoping it was accidental death. One murder was enough to worry about."

"I told you there was somethin' funny about that one."

"I hope you don't find any more funny ones for a while," Charles said somberly.

The two men sat silently, each thinking his own thoughts until the jingle of the telephone interrupted.

"Sheriff Matthews," Charles said. Two vertical lines of anger appeared between his eyebrows.

"Why didn't the idiot report it?" The answer appeared to increase Charles's anger. "We'll be right out, Raul. Don't let that fool get away."

Charles slammed the receiver down and grabbed his hat. Jamming it on his head, he stomped to the door, angrily jerking it open. "Which one of you talked to the airport manager yesterday?"

Mabel Honeycutt, the dispatcher, and Slim turned to the sheriff. Slim noisily cleared his throat. Someone was in a damn lot of trouble, and it appeared to be him.

"I did, Sheriff. He called about seven o'clock, and I was already here. Wasn't any use in one of the night-shift boys working overtime, so I chased out there. Someone had taken a spray plane out joyriding. I took a look around but didn't see anything except a jimmied lock on the hangar. The plane was parked at the end of the runway. It wasn't hurt or nothin', so I just came back and wrote up a report."

"Did it every occur to you that we were looking for a spray plane that dumped parathion on Billy Joe Williams? Now, don't you think I might have been interested in knowing about a joyride in a spray plane on Sunday morning?"

"Well, Sheriff," Slim said nervously, "I did write up a report and put it on your desk."

"You're right, Slim; I should have read the report. And I should have checked the dispatcher's log. But when it became obvious I had done neither, I would think you would have had enough sense to bring it to my attention. More such stupidity on your part, and you'll find yourself mopping out the drunk tank with that garbage you call coffee. Do you understand me?"

"Yes, sir." Slim gulped, wondering how anybody could sound so mean without ever raising his voice.

"I want you to listen very carefully to what I'm about to say, Slim: Billy Joe Williams was murdered. So was the victim in the barbecue pit. Now, Meenie and I are going out to the

airport. If anybody calls with any information about either of
those murders, or anything at all unusual, even if it doesn't
have to do with the cases, you call me over the radio. Do you
understand me, Slim?''

"Yes, sir," Slim said, standing at attention, his face so
white his freckles stood out like paint dabs.

"Good! I'm glad to hear it. Come on, Meenie.'' Charles
headed for the elevator, anger evident in every line of the lithe,
broad-shouldered body. Meenie wisely kept silent, listening to
the sheriff berate both himself and Slim. The short ride to the
airport was accomplished before Charles had finished his ti-
rade.

The Crawford County airport was typical of most small-
town Panhandle airports: two runways, crossing in an X pat-
tern, long corrugated metal hangars rented by private pilots,
next to a series of similar hangars where the various aerial
spraying services were housed. A small frame building to the
west of the hangars served as an office and flight center, if a
two-way radio, a battered desk, a bathroom, and an old vinyl
couch could be considered a flight center.

Raul was standing in front of a hangar whose roof was
emblazoned with the words Gentry's Flying Service. He broke
off his conversation with a tall man whose arms were making
windmill motions in the air and walked over to meet Charles
and Meenie. "I've got Red Turner, airport manager, Russell
Gentry, the owner of the spray plane, and Jim Everett, the kid
that was on duty yesterday morning, over in the hangar.''
Raul's eyes narrowed at the sight of the sheriff's face. He
could remember his old parish priest having that same expression whenever he caught a boy who didn't know his catechism.
Raul glanced at Meenie, who silently mouthed, "later.''

Charles strolled up to the airport manager and shook his
hand. "Red, I'm sorry it's taken so long for me to get out here,
but I've been a little busy.'' Charles's effortless charm didn't
seem to mollify the annoyed manager.

"Well, Sheriff, I know you're a busy man, but someone's
stealing a spray plane is pretty serious business.'' The manager
stuck his chin out belligerently.

"I know it, Red—particularly when that spray plane may be involved in a murder."

"A murder! Now just a dang minute, Sheriff. Just how was my plane involved?" A tall, whipcord-lean figure of a man demanded in a nasal drawl.

"Someone dumped a load of parathion on Billy Joe Williams yesterday," replied Charles.

"Well, it wasn't my plane. I just cleaned the tanks out Saturday, after my last spraying job. You can't leave those chemicals in the tanks overnight, they'll congeal, and then you've got a damn mess." The owner appeared pleased at being one up on the sheriff.

"Suppose we check the tanks, Mr. Gentry. Where's the plane?"

"Right in this hanger, Sheriff. I haven't flown it today; the wind's too damn strong to spray.

The sheriff walked over to the yellow plane with its broad, heavy wings. He looked at it helplessly, realizing he didn't have the slightest idea how to check the tanks. Charles, unlike many Panhandle residents, didn't have a private pilot's license. A plane was something he sat in while somebody else did the flying.

"Check the tanks, please, Mr. Gentry. I'm afraid I don't know much about spray planes." Charles gracefully confessed his own ignorance.

"It's a waste of time, Sheriff. But if it'll make you happy." Mr. Gentry unscrewed the cap from one of the tanks. The strong, unmistakable smell of parathion rose in the air. Cursing, Mr. Gentry ran around the plane and checked the other tank. Hurrying out of the hangar, he check his supply of parathion. He came back, angrier than before. "I take it back, Sheriff; someone did fill the tanks. I'll fix that idiot when I catch him. That stuff is expensive and dangerous."

"Is it difficult to fill the tanks? Would a person need specialized knowledge?" asked Charles.

"Hell, no; anybody could fill those tanks; even you could do it. It's a little harder to fly it; the wings are heavier than most small planes."

"Could any pilot fly it?"

"I suppose they could; a plane is a plane. But I wouldn't want somebody with no experience flying my plane."

"Meenie, get the fingerprint kit out of the car and get to work on that plane. Maybe there's a strange print somewhere. Mr. Gentry, we'll need to take prints from everybody that's ever been near that plane, for comparison."

"I don't let anybody near that plane except myself, my other pilot, and Red here. That's what makes me so damn mad about this; I don't like people messing around my plane."

"I don't blame you, Mr. Gentry. Now, what is your name?" Charles turned to the teenager.

"Jim Everett, sir," the boy replied, eyeing Charles curiously. The highly polished boots and Stetson were the only western items about the sheriff's appearance. Ordinary slacks and sports jacket, a shirt and tie were definitely not the average dress for a Panhandle sheriff. One end of a piece of thick leather was tucked in the breast pocket of his shirt. On the other end hanging outside the pocket was the familiar star-shaped badge of a western sheriff. It was the only indication that Charles was anything other than an urban businessman slumming in the country.

Charles smiled at the boy's expression. He realized he didn't fit the mold of a county sheriff. "Now, Jim, suppose you tell me everything that happened Sunday morning."

The boy glanced uneasily at the airport manager. "Well, sir, I got here a little after six; I was late," he said. "I saw the hangar was open but didn't think too much about it. Mr. Gentry starts spraying before six o'clock lots of times. I opened up the office and checked to see if there were any messages about special chores I needed to do. There weren't, so I swept the floor and sort of straightened everything up. It was a few minutes later that I heard the plane. I glanced out the window just in time to see it land. I went outside to see if Mr. Gentry needed any help, but the plane taxied all the way to the end of the runway and stopped. I saw the door open and someone jump out. I was too far away to see who it was, but I knew it wasn't Mr. Gentry."

"How did you know that, Jim?" Charles interrupted.

"Well, he was too short; he must have been three or four inches shorter than Mr. Gentry," the boy replied.

"How do you know he was shorter if you were too far away to recognize him?"

"By where his head came to on the plane. That's when I decided something was wrong. I yelled and started running toward the plane. The man saw me and started to run, too. He ran into that corn patch and drove away. I didn't see him do that, but I could hear the motor. I went back to the office and called the manager. He and Mr. Gentry got here fifteen or twenty minutes later. I think Red called your office. Anyway, a deputy came out, wrote down our story, said he would keep in touch, and left. If I had been on time, I would have caught the guy."

"If you had been on time, Jim, you would have been killed, and I would have three bodies instead of two," Charles said. He stood watching Meenie meticulously dust the plane with fingerprint powder. "Find anything yet, Meenie?"

"No, just one clear set in the door, the instrument panel, the steering wheel or whatever you call it, and the wings. Everything else is either wiped clean or is so smudged the prints are useless."

Charles, waiting for Meenie to finish it, listened to the two men and the boy speculate on the identity of the spray plane thief.

"Hell, I know plenty of people who would steal my plane just to get my goat, but none of them would have any reason to kill Billy Joe Williams," Gentry said. "Billy Joe was as useless as a milk bucket under a bull, but that's no reason to kill a man. If that was all it took, the undertakers would run out of caskets in an hour."

Charles overheard the comment and silently agreed. Billy Joe was not worth killing unless he were a threat to someone alive. Jerking his head to one side, he motioned Raul to the edge of the hangar. "Did you find out anything about the men on the list?"

"Yes, only three men on your list have pilot's licenses: Jim Bob Brown, Leon McDaniels, and your old friend Sammy the J.P."

"I'm surprised that tub of lard could climb in a small plane, much less pilot one."

"Sammy has more hours logged at this airport than anyone else in town. The manager says he's a good pilot."

"I'm glad to hear Sammy is good at something; he certainly isn't worth much as a J.P. What about Jim Bob Brown?"

"Jim Bob ran a spraying service about fifteen years ago down in Hereford."

"Why didn't you tell me when I gave the list to you?"

"Because I didn't know it. The manager told me. He also told me he didn't think Jim Bob had been up in a plane for the last four or five years."

"He might have decided to reacquaint himself with spray planes. He doesn't have an alibi for Saturday night."

"I don't think he was faking his reaction to finding the body, Sheriff."

"Perhaps his reaction was to the fact that there was a body to find. Whoever placed that body in the barbecue pit expected it to be destroyed. Yes, I think we'll look more closely at Jim Bob Brown. He's a lot brighter than he acts. Now, what about Leon McDaniels?"

"Mr. McDaniels can pilot a spray plane, and does a lot of his own spraying."

"Then he needs to be investigated on two counts," said Charles pensively.

"What do you mean?" Raul asked, a puzzled frown on his face.

"Maria Martinez's father works for him; in fact, they live on the McDaniels's property."

"What does Maria's father have to do with the case?"

"We think the body is, or was, I should say, Maria Martinez."

"Little Maria! *Madre de Dios!*"

"Yes. Dr. Akin said the body was that of a young girl who had broken her left leg. Plus, Maria was reported missing by her brother and her whole family."

"He works for Mr. Gentry," Raul said.

"Who does? Mr. Martinez?"

"No, Roberto Martinez. He is the only other pilot that Gentry has any use for. Roberto's been with him the last eight years. Went to work right after he came home from Vietnam."

"My God!" Charles said. "Another man who knew the victim and has flown a spray plane."

"Her own brother, Sheriff! You can't suspect him. He was proud of his sister."

"I suspect everybody, Raul. If you could fly a spray plane, I'd give you the third degree."

"I'm glad I can't." Raul smiled, wiping his hand across his forehead with a dramatic gesture. The two men stood in companionable silence for a few minutes. "Why would anyone want to kill Maria?" Raul asked sadly. "She seemed to be a nice enough girl."

"I don't know," said Charles. "I want you with me when I go out there tomorrow. Maybe her family will be more candid with you."

"I doubt it, Sheriff. I'm not really one of them. I'm a native-born citizen with no family ties to Mexico; in fact, I've never even been there. That almost makes me an Anglo."

"But Mr. Martinez has lived here for years. Most of his children were born here," Charles objected.

"But he has family in Mexico; they used to go back to visit them. Also, they still speak Spanish in the home. They're like a lot of immigrant families, Sheriff. They see Mexico as a place in which they belonged. They forget the poverty, disease, and unemployment. They feel out of place here so they cling harder to the customs of their homeland. I'll go with you; at least I speak the language better than you. But I don't think they will trust me any more than you."

"Okay, Raul. I'll just use you as a translator." Charles walked back to the plane. "You about through, Meenie?"

Meenie's grizzled head peered at the sheriff over one of the wings. "Just about. I used up all the fingerprint powder, but I think I covered everything." His bowlegged figure detoured over to the door of the hangar, and Charles heard the familiar hawking sound that accompanied one of Meenie's more ambitious expectorations. He walked back to the sheriff, a beatific expression on his face. Charles wondered if Meenie had hit a flying grasshopper at fifty paces. Unable to stop himself, he asked, "What did you hit?"

"Damn beetle I began watching crawl all over the hangar. Hit him just before he disappeared into a crack. Must have been ten, maybe fifteen feet away."

"Dammit, finish your job and spit at beetles later," Charles ordered. He was hot, tired, and faced a hell of a day tomorrow. A J.P., a county commissioner, and one of the richest farmer-ranchers in the Panhandle were to be questioned about a murder.

The three men crisscrossed through the tall rows of corn searching for footprints. Young Jim stood on the edge of the runway, his whole body expressing his disappointment at being told not to step off the asphalt.

"Did you find anything, Sheriff?" he yelled, excitement at being this close to a real murder case causing him to rock back and forth on his boots.

"That's got to be the tenth time that kid has asked the same question," Meenie muttered. A muffled exclamation caused him to hurry over to the sheriff, carefully examining the ground before putting his feet down. Meenie hunkered down beside the sheriff and Raul. There it was: a single bootprint, the toe deeper than the heel. "Looks like he was running, don't it?" asked Meenie.

"Jim said he was running," the sheriff replied, rising to slide between the rows of corn in search of another print. The trio followed the row of footprints to a narrow dirt track, barely wide enough for a vehicle, that divided the field into two sections. Broken stalks, their weighty ears of corn resting on the ground, bore witness to a vehicle having backed over them to turn around. The twin tracks of the road were dry and dusty. The Panhandle wind had been an unwitting friend to the murderer. While the tire tracks were still visible, the loose dirt had been blown about, making their imprint unsuitable for identification.

Cursing audibly and mutinously, Charles walked down the track, searching for some spot where the tire prints might be more vivid. His two deputies followed him, silent in the face of his rising frustration. Charles seldom indulged in the casual profanity that often colored local conversation. To hear him do it now was a shock. Meenie cleared this throat and spat, for once not looking for a specific target. "Sheriff, it's just too dry and windy. We got a pretty clear footprint only because he ran between the stalks where the ground is loose and sorta protected, but even it ain't worth much for identification. No sense beatin' a dead horse. We ain't goin' to get any casts of tire tracks."

The sheriff stopped and, turning, began to run back toward the runway. He stopped at the broken stalks of corn and carelessly tossed them aside. "Dammit, Meenie, you're brilliant, absolutely brilliant," he panted.

Meenie took his hat off and, pulling out a handkerchief, wiped the bald circle at the crown of his head. He didn't feel brilliant; in fact, he couldn't figure out what he had said that caused the sheriff to nose around in the corn like a prairie dog diggin' a new tunnel.

Charles's shout of triumph brought his deputies scurrying over. There beneath the sheltering broken stalks were two tire tracks, indelibly stamped in the loose soil.

"Well, I'll be damned," Meenie said. "I never thought of that, Sheriff."

"Raul, have you ever made a plaster cast of a tire print?" the sheriff asked.

Raul shook his head. "I've made casts of figures for kids to paint, and my wife has taught some ceramics, but I've never done anything like this. Training school covered it, but I've never had any practical experience."

Meenie held up his hands in a mock attempt to ward off the sheriff's eagerness. "I've never done it either, Sheriff; Crawford County just don't run to fancy detective work. Training schools are all right, but they sure don't beat firsthand experience."

Charles pounded his knee in frustration. To call in someone from Amarillo or the Department of Public Safety to make the cast might take days. In the meantime, the wind might destroy the print. A guard would have to be posted to protect it. Damn, what he wouldn't give for a really good lab, or at least a fully trained technician. His brows drew together thoughtfully. "Raul, could your wife make a cast for us?"

"Yes, I'm sure she could."

"Good!" said Charles, feeling one less problem weighing on his mind. "Call her, will you? Have one of the deputies pick her up and run her out here. Meenie and I are going in to see Billy Joe's mother."

Clasping Raul's shoulder for a moment, he wheeled and jerked his head at Meenie. The tall rows of corn swayed behind the men's retreating backs.

# CHAPTER

# 6

"CRAWFORD THIRTY-TWO, COME IN." CHARLES clicked on his receiver in the patrol car.

"Thirty-two, go ahead." Mabel's voice squealed over the radio, high, shrill, and nasal all at the same time.

".I'll be at Mrs. Williams's on Laredo Street. Call me there if anything happens."

"What's the number, Sheriff?" asked the dispatcher.

"I don't know, but I'm sure it's in the phone book. You know what a phone book is?"

"Of course, Sheriff." The voice sounded hurt.

"Then look it up!" the sheriff snapped. "Thirty-two, ten-four. Damn, what does that woman use for brains?"

"I don't rightly know, Sheriff, but I think she was issued along with the radio equipment back in the forties. She's the only one who can keep it running. If you fire Mabel, you're gonna have to talk the county commissioners into buying a new base unit." Meenie turned his head and spat out the window. Charles shuddered. Any car that Meenie drove always ended up with brown streaks down the side.

"I'm not looking forward to this," said Charles.

"She's a good woman, Sheriff; her only blind spot was Billy Joe."

Meenie stopped the patrol car in front of a small white frame house badly in need of paint. Flower beds filled with brilliantly colored petunias ran the length of the house on either side of the front porch.

A jolly woman with determinedly black hair and grizzled eyebrows opened the door. "Meenie, you back again?" she asked, sparkling black eyes looking over Meenie's shoulder to the sheriff. She patted her stiffly lacquered hair and smiled flirtatiously.

"Sheriff, this is Mrs. Jameson; she lives next door and came to stay with Mrs. Williams. Mrs. Williams ain't got any kin."

Charles smiled at Mrs. Jameson and shook her hand. "I'm sure Mrs. Williams must appreciate having such a good neighbor."

"Oh, Lord, I'm more than a neighbor. Ginny and I grew up together. Always at one another's house, we were. Of course, you wouldn't know we were the same age to look at us now. Ginny has just plain let herself go. A woman oughten to do that. Now me, I'm going to stay young looking as long as I can." Mrs. Jameson patted her hair again.

Charles's lip twitched momentarily. "You're doing an admirable job of it, too, Mrs. Jameson. You certainly don't look a day over thirty-five," Charles lied, finding the woman's posturing harmless and rather humorous.

"Now, Sheriff, you're teasing me. Don't try to deny it; I know you are." Charles watched in astonishment as Mrs. Jameson actually wagged her finger at him.

"Every attractive woman should expect a little teasing," Charles said gallantly. "But Mrs. Jameson, we need to see Mrs. Williams. Is she able to answer some questions?"

"Oh, I think so, Sheriff; she's feeling much better today. I went with her to the funeral home to view the body. He looked so natural. It's so miraculous what undertakers can do these days."

Charles kept his expression bland and interested. In his experience, dead bodies usually looked dead. And he didn't see how viewing one's own son in a casket could possibly make one feel better.

"Don't you agree, Sheriff?" Mrs. Jameson asked.

"Oh, I'm sorry; I didn't hear the question." Charles was embarrassed.

"I said that having all the arrangements made for a funeral, and seeing the deceased looking so peaceful, always makes a person feel better." Mrs. Jameson waited for his reply with bated breath.

Charles, feeling he had listened to all the clichés about funerals he could stand in one conversation, smiled. "That's certainly one opinion. Now, if you would tell Mrs. Williams we're here, I would certainly appreciate it."

"I'll go get her, Sheriff. She's just back in the bedroom with her feet up. She looked a little peaked when we got back from the funeral home, so I told her to take a rest before supper. Now you just sit down, Sheriff; I'll go call her." Her three chins jiggling merrily, Mrs. Jameson disappeared through a door.

Blonde hair and blue eyes must have made Billy Joe's mother a striking beauty as a girl; now she merely looked colorless and nondescript. Her dress was a shirtwaist of the cheapest sort, and the seams showed the wear of repeated washings. A plain gold band was worn on her left hand, a band that obviously could not be removed over the swollen knuckles.

Charles rose to his feet and took Mrs. Williams's hand. "I'm sorry to bother you at a time like this, but we need to know about Billy Joe." He patted the slender hand, feeling calluses and swollen joints. "Mrs. Jameson, if you would excuse us, please?" he asked, leading Mrs. Wiliams over to the couch.

Mrs. Jameson looked startled for a moment, then smiled in understanding. She winked broadly at the sheriff, and Charles cringed inwardly. "I'll just run next door for a minute, Ginny; you call me when the sheriff leaves. I'm sure you'll want to talk to him alone." With that, she left the house, waving her fingers at the sheriff.

"Bertha comes on a little strong, but she means well," Mrs. Williams said in a faint voice. "I've known her all my life, and I had no one else to turn to when my poor baby was killed." Charles had a mental image of a grown Billy Joe with a baby's bonnet on his head, drinking his beer from a bottle.

"Mrs. Williams, I would rather do anything than what I am about to do. I've always wished there was some magic way to say this that wouldn't cause pain, but there isn't. Billy Joe was murdered."

Mrs. Williams's faded blue eyes looked into the sheriff's brown ones, then skittered away. She seemed to shrink a little, as though some substance had leaked away.

"I think I knew that deep inside. Nothing else made any sense." Her voice was as thin as her body.

"Mrs. Williams, you must have had a good reason for believing that. Please tell me what it was." Charles waited, but she sat quietly, seeming not to hear him. He touched her arm. "Tell me what happened when Billy Joe came home Saturday night. I want you to describe everything he did and said. Would you do that for me, please?" Charles nodded imperceptibly at Meenie, a signal to take notes.

Mrs. Williams sat quietly, a single tear rolling down her cheek. Charles felt a pity so deep, his own eyes burned from the pressure of unshed tears. There was something so sorrowful about that single tear, unaccompanied by any sound. He wondered if he were suited for his job, and if his objectivity had been forever shattered by the events in Dallas. He jerked slightly when Mrs. Williams began to speak.

"I'll tell you, Sheriff, but I'm not very good at describing things. Billy Joe came in about midnight. I was still awake; I had pulled some weeds out of my garden, and my hands were hurting so badly I couldn't sleep. I have arthritis in my hands and arms. It's hard sometimes to do what needs to be done." She shook her head slightly and veered back to the subject.

"I heard Billy Joe open the refrigerator and take out a can of beer. I don't really approve of drinking, but a man likes his beer. I got up to hear how his evening went, and knocked one of my little figurines off the table. I guess it must have startled him. He jerked around to look at me, and his face was white as a sheet. He was scared, Sheriff, real scared; I never saw my boy so scared. He said, 'Dammit, Ma, don't creep up on me like that.'

"I asked him what was wrong, but he wouldn't talk about anything. He finished his beer and got another can. He got mad because our refrigerator is old and doesn't keep the beer as cold as he likes it. He said we needed a new one. I agreed but told him we just couldn't afford it. Then he started in about his pickup; he wanted a new one. I finally just let him talk. I felt bad because I couldn't give him some of the things he wanted."

Her voice trailed off, and she pulled a crumbled handkerchief out of her pocket. She wiped her eyes and drew a deep breath, her swollen hands nervously folding the piece of cloth. Charles wanted to comfort her by saying he was sure Billy Joe understood, but the words wouldn't come. Charles leaned closer as the thin voice continued.

"Billy Joe walked up and down the living room, drinking his beer. This is an old house, and there was a strong wind blowing that night. Each time the house creaked, Billy Joe would jump out of his skin. Finally, close to two o'clock, he told me to go to bed; he needed to make a phone call and wanted privacy. The phone's right here by the couch and my bedroom is on the other side of the wall. I could hear some of the conversation. Someone answered the phone, and Billy Joe told whoever it was he had some information for sale. There was silence, then I heard Billy Joe say something about a tailwater pit out on 1283.

"I didn't hear anything else for a while. Then I heard Billy Joe cursing. He said he wasn't going to give his name, that he wasn't a fool. Then he started cursing again, and I heard him tell someone not to hang up, that he meant business. There was silence for a long time. Finally, I heard Billy Joe ask where did he want to meet. I never knew who he was talking to, or where the meeting was going to be, or anything else. I heard Billy Joe say that was okay, and then he hung up."

Her voice faded. She clasped the sheriff's arm with one swollen hand. "I'll always blame myself for not going out there and telling Billy Joe not to go anywhere." Mrs. Williams began crying again, the tears seeping through the fingers she pressed against her eyes.

Charles wished Billy Joe was still alive so he could have the privilege of kicking his butt all the way around the courthouse. Drawing on the last reserves of compassion, he reached out and patted the old woman's shoulders. "You're looking at the situation from hindsight. You had no way of knowing exactly what Billy Joe was talking about. Even if you had talked to him, I doubt he would have listened. We all have a tendency to blame ourselves when someone dies, or to feel guilty because our last thoughts of them were angry or disdainful. You always did the best you could for Billy Joe; no one could ask for more." Charles hated himself for his hypocrisy. He wanted to scream what now seemed obvious: that Billy Joe had seen something he wasn't meant to, thought he'd found an easy way to make some money from it, and he had been too stupid to realize blackmail was dangerous.

Mrs. Williams blew her nose on the oft-folded handkerchief and dabbed at her streaming eyes. "Thank you, Sheriff."

"What time did Billy Joe leave, Mrs. Williams?"

"I don't know. I was going to stay awake, to talk to him, but I was so tired, I fell asleep. When I woke up about six, Billy Joe was gone. Who killed my boy, Sheriff?" Her red-veined eyes were beseeching. "He was a good boy."

Charles wondered momentarily what her definition of a bad boy would be. Love may be blind, but in her case, braille wouldn't even help. "I don't know, Mrs. Williams, but I will." His tone of voice made those words a vow.

# CHAPTER

# 7

"CHARLES, HAVE YOU EATEN ANYTHING TODAY?" Angie's voice was touched with concern.

Charles feasted his eyes on her face with its wide-set hazel eyes and laughing mouth. It was not a beautiful face. The chin was too square, the nose a little too short; but taken altogether, it was an attractive one. Charles felt helpless against his feelings for her. Striving for a lightness of mood he didn't feel, he ruffled the chestnut brown curls and avoided her eyes.

"I grabbed a burger on the way over, Angie. But some tea would be fine."

"There's some beer. Would you rather have that?" she asked, smiling affectionately at him.

Charles rubbed his stomach where the familiar burning caused by too little sleep and too many unremitting demands on his emotions was beginning. He knew a beer would only add to the discomfort facing him. "No, just tea. Too much beer is bad for the waistline."

Angie glanced enviously at the lean body of the man in front of her. "All right, tea it is." She turned to her husband. "Do you want a beer, L.D.?"

"No, I've already made myself a drink." L.D.'s voice was preoccupied.

Charles raised an eyebrow. L.D. seldom drank anything stronger than a beer. "You okay, L.D.?" he asked.

L.D. took a large swallow of his drink and set it down hard enough to cause the liquid to slosh over the sides of the glass. "No, I'm not okay. I find a dead body this morning; I saw a dead boy yesterday you tell me was murdered. The murderer is probably going to be somebody I know, grew up with, and you ask me if I'm okay!'' L.D.'s voice rose to almost a shout. He raked a hand through his sandy hair.

"I'm sorry; I know it's tougher for you than it is for me. It's going to be even worse. The body was Maria Martinez.''

The glass dropped from L.D.'s nerveless fingers, shattering on the tiled kitchen floor. Angie gasped, color fading from her cheeks.

"My God!'' L.D. swore. Angie turned her back to the men, her head thrown back, throat moving convulsively in an attempt not to cry.

"How do you know?'' L.D. demanded. "You can't be sure—I mean, the body was pretty badly burned. Besides, Maria is not the kind of girl to get herself murdered. You're wrong; it can't be Maria.''

"Roberto brought the family in this afternoon to report her missing. The body is the right age, the right sex, and had had a broken left leg, just like Maria. I sent the X-rays over to Dr. Akin, but I'm afraid it's just a formality. The body is Maria's.''

Angie's shoulders shook with sobs, but L.D. stared vacantly ahead, ignoring her. Charles turned her around and pulled her against his chest, clumsily patting her back. "Come on, Angie girl, it's all right,'' he murmured.

He started to say something to L.D., but stopped. He lifted her head to wipe the tears away with his fingertips.

Angie pulled away and angrily wiped at her eyes. "I'm sorry, Charles. I don't know what got into me. I didn't really know the girl that well. She stayed with the kids overnight a couple of times, and she worked after school for L.D. I guess that it's just so horrible to know someone who was murdered, plus having her found in such a place. L.D. would say I was being too emotional again.''

Charles felt the wet splotches on his shirt from Angie's tears. His skin seemed to burn each place they had touched. "Why shouldn't you be emotional about the girl's death. You knew her, after all.''

"My God, Charles, I still can't believe it!'' L.D. exclaimed. "Friday she was talking about her plans after the barbecue.

She was just a happy, typical teenager. Why in hell would anyone want to kill her?''

"I don't know, L.D.," Charles said wearily. "That's one of the things I'm hoping to find out."

"She wasn't typical, you know," Angie said slowly. Both men turned to her in surprise. "She was very mature for her age and had plans for going to college. Her family couldn't afford to send her, and they were upset at her wanting a career instead of marrying and staying here. She was very strong willed to go against her family and cultural traditions. I asked her if she were going to apply for scholarships to college. She told me she was, but that she also had found someone who would help her. I was a little uneasy when she told me that; she was a beautiful girl, and I was afraid the someone might be a man who would have quite a price tag on his help. Also, she was a natural flirt, who was totally unaware of it."

"Angie! That doesn't sound like Maria. She was a nice kid, and one of the smartest vocational students who ever worked in my office, but I certainly never saw her as a flirt," L.D. said.

Angie smiled helplessly at her husband's outrage. "Oh, I don't mean it in a derogatory way. There was nothing cold or calculating about Maria. She just related easily to men. Someone misunderstood. Maybe when Maria refused to go to bed with him, he killed her."

"Oh, for God's sake, Angie!" L.D. said. "There are plenty of women giving it away for free. Why should anyone kill for it?"

Angie flushed at the crudeness of L.D.'s remark.

"Stop!" Charles shouted. Two pairs of startled eyes turned to look at him. "Sorry, Angie, L.D.; I didn't mean to yell. It's just that I was feeling cocky about solving this murder by investigating the characters of the suspects. Now you've reminded me that the victims, or at least one victim, needs to be investigated, too." Charles ran his fingers through his hair in frustration. "It never stops in a small town, does it? This interdependence, this knowledge of one another that ties you all together. Am I going to find anybody that doesn't know the victims?"

"I doubt it, Charles," Angie said softly. "The town just isn't that big. Twelve thousand people isn't very many." She touched his arm. "Go in the living room and relax. I'll get your tea."

He had barely sat down when the phone rang. Wearily, he pulled himself back up and headed for the kitchen. Angie's clear voice telling the caller to wait a minute answered his unasked question. She silently handed him the phone, sympathy in her eyes. He rubbed the back of his neck, trying to relieve the tightness.

"Hello." Abruptly he straightened, the tired lines of his face smoothing out as if a hand wiped his face clean. "When did he call?" Charles demanded. "Okay, I'll call him right back."

Charles hung the receiver up and pulled out his billfold. "Angie," he asked over his shoulder, "do you mind if I make a credit card call?"

"No, Charles. Is it something personal? Would you like to use the phone in the bedroom?"

"Yes, if I may," he answered. He followed Angie through the kitchen and down a hall into the master bedroom. A queen-sized bed with a gold spread stood against one wall. Angie pointed to the princess phone on a bedside table and quietly left the room, closing the door.

Charles held the phone stiffly in his hand, counting the number of rings. Finally, a tired voice answered. "Dr. Akin, this is Sheriff Matthews; my office said you had called."

"Young man, you got a mean one running around loose; I hope you can catch him in a hurry."

"What do you mean?" Charles asked, feeling his palms start to sweat.

"I mean the head injury didn't kill that girl; she died of smoke inhalation. She was still alive when she went into that pit. I'm not saying she would have lived anyway, but she damn sure had a chance. Thanks to the way the body was curled up and the fact that there was dirt piled on top, I found some of one lung intact. It's damn hard to burn a human body."

"Couldn't the smoke have entered the lungs after she was dead, and the fire lit?" Charles asked. The thought of someone disposing of a living body so callously made him nauseous.

"No, young man, it could not. The only way smoke can get in the lungs is for someone to inhale. In order to inhale, you have to be alive."

"Perhaps the murderer thought the girl was dead," said Charles.

"I wouldn't know about that," Dr. Akin said testily. "Autopsies don't reveal what people thought, only what they did. By the way, I think I solved your problem of motive: the girl was pregnant. I also compared the X-rays with the girl's leg; it was Maria Martinez. I'll send you a complete report on both bodies in the morning. You got a cold-blooded killer running around, son, and I sure as hell hope nobody else gets in his way. I don't want another body from Crawford County for a while; I'm ready to go back to simple knivings and shootings."

"Thanks, Dr. Akin. I appreciate your working overtime to get those autopsies done."

"It's my job, son, and I'd rather have it than yours. Call me again if you have any more questions." The doctor hung up and Charles sat looking at the phone, feeling numb all over.

He hung it up and wiped his hands on his slacks. Each new bit of information made the case more horrifying than the last. Suddenly he wanted to get out, go back to his office where he would think through the whole thing.

He walked back to the living room and halted in the doorway. "I'm going, L.D., Angie. Thanks for the tea and the use of your telephone."

"Who called, Charles?" L.D. asked, observing the pallor of his friend's face.

"Dr. Akin finished the autopsy, L.D. I had to talk to him about the results." His mind was already seeking an escape from his friends' concern.

"What could he possibly tell you that could upset you so badly, Charles?" Angie asked, coming up to touch his arm.

Charles looked into her face, wishing she was his to soothe him.

"Maria was pregnant," he said bluntly.

Angie put her hand over her mouth, her eyes going round with shock. "Oh, no!"

"There's your motive," L.D. said. "Someone killed her to keep her from talking."

Charles shook his head. "No one kills a girl just because he gets her pregnant; not in this day and time."

He hugged Angie briefly and raised his hand in a gesture of farewell to L.D. He let their protests to his leaving lap over him as he continued to the front door and out to his patrol car.

Settling himself in the patrol car, he flipped on the radio. Almost immediately the familiar code was broadcast. "Crawford thirty-two, go ahead." Slim's drawl came over the radio, and Charles wondered idly what he was still doing at the courthouse; his shift was over at four o'clock.

"Sheriff, we got a problem with Old Ben. He wants to be locked up, but he ain't drunk. What am I supposed to do?"

"Give him a cup of coffee and find him a place to sit down. I'll be there in a minute."

"Sheriff, Old Ben says he hasn't drunk anything without whiskey in it for fifty years. Says coffee's bad for the digestion."

"If he's speaking of the brew at the Crawford County Jail, he's right. Add a dash of liquor from the jug, and give it to him."

"If you say so, Sheriff," Slim said doubtfully.

"I say so. Ten-four," Charles said. He hung up the mike and thought about Old Ben. He wore cast-off clothes and eked out a meager existence on Social Security. Tall, skeletal-thin, with most of his teeth missing, Ben was as much a mystery after twenty years as he was the day he arrived in Carroll. He had looked old and ill then, and he had not changed over the years. Periodically the welfare agencies would attempt to confine him to a nursing home, but Old Ben would make it back to the boxcar shanty where he lived before the social worker could finish her paperwork. Completely independent, Old Ben continued in his chosen life-style, alone except for a white, skinny, miserable-looking mutt that followed him around.

Toward the end of each month Old Ben would show up at the courthouse noticeably drunk. Charles would file charges on him, and the county judge would obligingly sentence Old Ben to ten days in jail. Assured of a warm place to sleep and three meals a day, he would settle down happily in the corner cell where he could watch the downtown streets. Charles occasionally dropped in to visit him, but only after the jailer had given Old Ben his monthly bath. He was surprised to find the old man a superior chess player, and the two men played several games each month.

Charles often wondered about him—who he was, where he came from, but most of all, what had happened to him. Old Ben always smiled at Charles's questions, but he never answered. His reticence was more than a shield, it was an impenetrable wall. Only one time during the last two years had he ever answered a question even indirectly. His faded blue eyes had peered slyly at Charles and his toothless mouth had grinned. "Sometimes, Sheriff, life can get to be too much." He had reached over, made a move, and announced, "Checkmate," leaving Charles staring foolishly at the chessboard.

Charles locked the patrol car and walked up the steps to the dark courthouse. Fitting his key in the door, he paused to watch the carnival. Frontier Days was in full swing, and he thought of L.D.'s mention of Maria having plans for the barbecue.

Charles relocked the courthouse door and took the elevator to the third story, where the Crawford County Sheriff's Department shared space with the county jail and the district courtroom. Stepping out of the elevator, he was assailed by the familiar mixture of scents that announced Old Ben's presence. The cheap liquor and strong tobacco weren't as strong this time, but then the old man had just been let out of jail a week before. Old Ben was ensconced on the cracked leather couch in the foyer, drinking his laced coffee, his little finger sticking straight out in exaggerated gentility.

Breathing shallowly, Charles stepped forward with outstretched hand. "Ben, what is this about wanting to go to jail?"

The old man remained huddled on the couch, ignoring the sheriff's hand. He looked up at Charles from beneath bushy brows. "I want you to lock me up." His voice sounded rusty, as if he weren't used to speaking.

"Now, Ben, I can't lock a man up for no reason. Why don't you let me buy you some dinner and take you home."

A spasm passed through the old man as though he were struck with a sudden chill. He licked his sunken lips for a moment. "What kind of a reason do you need, Sheriff?" he asked.

Charles was startled for a moment. "Well, Ben, we lock up people for all kinds of reasons. Drunkenness, but you're not drunk; violent crimes, like stealing or killing, or hitting someone, but you're not violent. So, I guess I'll just have to take you home," said Charles, reaching down to help the old man up.

Old Ben cringed away from Charles and rose shakily to his feet. He stumbled over to the dispatcher's desk where Slim stood watching, a coffeepot in one hand, a coffee can in the other. The old man stood trembling a moment, then doubled up his fist and hit Slim square on the chin. Slim's eyes rolled back in his head as he crumbled to the floor, coffeepot and coffee can going in different directions. The old man turned back to Charles, a sly grin of triumph exposing his toothless gums. "Is that enough to get a man locked up, Sheriff?"

# CHAPTER

# 8

"THE ONLY GOOD THING THAT HAPPENED YESTER-day was Slim's spilling so much coffee when he fell that I didn't have to eat my first cup with a spoon." Charles propped his feet up on top of his desk, and rubbed his red-rimmed eyes.

"Why do you suppose that old drunk wanted to be locked up so bad?" Meenie asked, leaning back in his usual chair and spitting in the general direction of the spitoon.

"I don't know, Meenie. I couldn't get a thing out of him. I just had the jailer lock him up."

"I don't understand it," Raul said. "Old Ben has never been violent."

Raul's voice went on, but Charles had stopped listening. Old Ben and his eccentric behavior was the least of his problems; he was more concerned with the murders. Fear had to be the reason for the murders. Fear of disclosure, then fear of discovery. Charles made a pyramid of his fingers, hooking the peak of it under his chin. He sighted along the toes of his boots as they rested on top of his desk. He had to know more, more about Maria and her relationship with men. If she had been sleeping with a man, someone had to know about it. A thing like that didn't stay a secret in Crawford County. A man didn't have time to get his pants zipped before the crowd at the doughnut shop was discussing his virility, his techniques, and his stamina.

Charles swung his feet off the desk and rose, rubbing his tired eyes again. After Old Ben had decked Slim, Charles had locked him up, then calmed his shaken deputy. It had been a short night, filled with nightmares. And he had a nagging feeling that he was forgetting something. He shook his head; perhaps it would come to him later.

"Raul, are you ready to question the Martinez family?"

"No, but I guess I'll have to, won't I?" replied the slim deputy.

"Yes, you will. Meenie, take a couple of deputies out and hit all the tailwater pits along 1283. Check for any signs of a struggle, any blood, any evidence at all that people had met there."

"My God, Sheriff, do you know how many tailwater pits there are on 1283? That whole section of the country is irrigated. It'll take days to check them all!" Meenie was clearly disgusted.

"Then take days! If it makes it any easier, start with the ones close to where Billy Joe was killed. And Meenie, don't take Slim; he can't find his own boots when they're on his feet. Now get going. Come on, Raul." Charles grabbed his hat off the filing cabinet and put in on.

"Mabel," he said to the dispatcher, "I'm going out to the Martinez place. I don't think they have a phone, so you'll have to send a car out if you need me."

"I'll just call you on the radio, Sheriff," Mabel's nasal voice answered.

Charles wondered if it were possible to talk the county commission out of a new communication system. "Mabel, I won't be sitting in the patrol car, I'll be in the house. Just send someone after me, will you?"

"Sheriff Johnson always interviewed people in his car if there wasn't a phone around," answered Mabel, a smug look on her face as she mentioned Charles's predecessor.

"Sheriff Johnson," Charles said through gritted teeth, "never had to interview the parents of a murder victim. I have no intention of subjecting them to that kind of treatment. Just send a car after me."

"Yes, Sheriff," Mabel said.

Charles stomped to the elevator, a thunderous expression on his face. He was still angry when he got into the patrol car and slammed the door. Damn, but he was going to get rid of that woman one way or another. "Sheriff Johnson was an incompetent," Charles exploded. "but you'd think he was God Almighty the way Mabel keeps quoting him."

"You have to remember that Sheriff Johnson held office over twenty years. A lot of the older deputies never worked under anyone else. It takes a while to change people's ways of doing things."

"They'd better change, or this new broom is going to start sweeping clean. Where is Leon McDaniels's place?" He grinned suddenly, his face looking younger, less tense. "That's really why I wanted you along. I still don't always know which wheat field or pasture belongs to whom. I would probably end up in the Oklahoma Panhandle if I tried to find the right cattle guard to turn on."

Charles sobered as he thought of the coming interviews. "Maria was pregnant, Raul. I think we'd better tell Roberto by himself. Let him tell the family when he thinks the time is right. We have to know who Maria was seeing because that person is automatically suspect."

"Roberto may not know, Sheriff. Her parents may not know. Her parents were very strict; I don't think she would have had the opportunity to be with anyone intimately enough to get pregnant if they had known."

"Good God! What kind of girl was she? Meenie tells me she was ambitious, Angie says she was a flirt who didn't know it, Roberto says she was a good girl, and now you tell me she was strictly raised and wouldn't be alone with a man long enough to become pregnant. Who was Maria Martinez?"

"Beautiful, smart, basically a good person, but young. The young make all kinds of mistakes to regret later."

"Angie says someone misunderstood Maria, that she was not a cold, calculating tease, but just got along better with men than women. Put that together with a seventeen-year-old's anxiety to try out her power, and you've got a potentially explosive situation."

Raul turned off 1283 and drove over a cattle guard, those uniquely western ditches covered over with iron bars. "Do those things really keep cattle in?" asked Charles curiously.

Raul shrugged. "I suppose so. That's all the ranchers around here use on their roads. I always thought cattle were dumb, but they're smart enough to know they can't walk across one of those things."

After about a quarter of a mile, Raul turned into a dirt driveway and stopped before a large, weathered frame house. A garden stretched out behind the house, and several cars were parked under the tall elm trees that shaded one side of the structure.

"It's the old McDaniels's homestead. When the big house was built, Leon gave this place to Mr. Martinez rent free."

Charles looked at the parked cars and drew a deep breath. "I guess we'd better get this over with," he said, reluctantly climbing out of the car. Setting his hat more firmly on his head, he walked toward the house, feeling the unseen eyes that must be watching him. He knocked on the door, his stomach beginning its familiar burning. He saw Raul from the corner of his eye and noticed his deputy's serious face. He focused his attention on the door and waited. He was beginning to shift uneasily and had raised his hand to knock again when Roberto opened the door.

"Sheriff," Roberto said. He stood in the door, making no gesture of welcome or invitation. Yet his home had always been Crawford County, and respect for institutions was a powerful force.

"Roberto, we have to ask you some questions," Charles said. "I can't find out who killed her unless I know the truth."

"What truth?" Roberto asked bitterly. "The truth is that someone killed her. Why are you asking questions about Maria?"

"Please," Charles said, motioning him outside. Roberto stood a moment longer, indecision stamped on his face. "Roberto, although your father is the head of your family, you are the one I must talk to. Come out here; I have to tell you something. You can tell your parents in whatever way and whatever time you think is best."

Roberto capitulated, stepping out and closing the door. "What do you want to tell me?" he asked, his defensiveness making his voice belligerent.

Charles hesitated, searching for the right words, the kind words, then he realized there weren't any. "The body was

Maria's. The X-rays of her leg and the one of the corpse were a perfect match. I'm sorry; I tried to prepare you yesterday." Charles looked discreetly at the fields while Roberto coped with his grief. After a few minutes, he continued. "We know more now than we did. We have the beginnings of a motive."

"What motive?" Roberto cried. "Why would anyone want to kill a child like Maria?"

"Maria was pregnant."

"Roberto lunged at him. "No! No! You are lying! You are trying to make Maria into a *puta*, a whore."

Raul's strong arms wrapped themselves around Roberto and lifted him bodily into the air. Muscles like thick ropes stood out in his shoulders and arms as he held the struggling man. *"Silencio!"* Raul hissed; *"Es verdad!"*

Roberto hung his head down, going limp in Raul's arms. *"No, no!"* he sobbed. *"No es verdad!"*

Charles took one of Roberto's arms and Raul the other as they seated the grieving man on the edge of the porch. They sat on the weathered boards on either side of the younger man. Charles put his arm around Roberto's shoulders and held him until the sobs lessened. Dropping his arm, the sheriff removed a clean handkerchief from his pocket and offered it to Roberto. Roberto raised his eyes to look at the sheriff. He saw only compassion and helplessness where he had expected impersonal sympathy or indifference. He took the handkerchief and blew his nose.

"It is true, isn't it, Sheriff?" Roberto asked dully. "Maria was pregnant?"

"Yes. I'm sorry. If I had thought the pregnancy had nothing to do with the murder, I wouldn't have told you."

"But how?" Roberto asked, never realizing the humor of his question. "My parents did not let her go out alone with boys; always there must be a friend along."

"Did she resent that, not being allowed to date like the other girls her age?" Charles asked, feeling sympathy for the beautiful young girl being raised by the standards of another culture, being set apart from her peers.

Roberto looked across the fields, not really wanting to reveal the family quarrels to any outsiders. "Yes," he said finally.

"She did not like it. I argued with my parents, but they were raising Maria as they had been raised. They did the same with my other sisters, but they did not seem to mind so much. And they are much older; it was different when they were young. Not so many of our boys had cars; there was not the money for dates. But now, it is better. Our men have good jobs and money. Our young people want to date like the Anglos." Roberto sat with his arms hanging between his legs, trying to accept what had happened to his sister and why.

"She must have met a man somewhere. Did she ever leave without telling your parents where she was going?"

"She often took walks in the evenings. I was always suspicious, but I had sorrow for her. I thought she was meeting a boy of her own age, and I saw nothing wrong. She wanted to be like everyone else. It is my fault, what happened to Maria; I should have told my parents."

"I can't tell you that you were wrong in not telling your parents. I probably would have done the same; I don't know. Did she ever talk about any men in general?"

"Yes, she talked about all the men in the courthouse. She talked about Mr. McDaniels. I don't remember one man more than another."

"Did she drive to school each day?"

"No, Maria did not know how to drive. She rode the bus to school, and I, or one of my brothers, would pick her up after work and bring her home. Sometimes she baby-sat for the Lassiters and Mr. Lassiter would bring her home. My parents wouldn't let her baby-sit for anyone else. Mrs. Lassiter would always ask my parents to let Maria stay with the children. My father liked that; he said it showed respect."

"Did she ever speak of Jim Bob Brown?"

Robert looked surprised. "Yes, of course. He was always teasing her. She liked him very much. Sometimes she worked for him, if Mr. Lassiter didn't need her."

Charles sat quietly, absorbing information that Maria had liked Jim Bob Brown. Obviously, he must have shown her a side that wasn't apparent to anybody else.

"What about the J.P.?" Charles asked.

"Maria didn't like him. I think she was afraid of him. Sometimes she would do some typing for him, but she did not like him. Once she came out of the courthouse and got in the car. She wouldn't talk to me, then she started crying. She told me she didn't want to work for him anymore. I was angry and drove back to town. I was going to tell him to leave my sister alone, but she begged me not to make trouble. She said she would just talk to Mr. Lassiter. She never worked for the J.P. again.''

"What about Mr. McDaniels? How did Maria feel about him?"

"Mr. McDaniels has been like a father to all of us. He taught me to fly, he helped my brothers and my sisters' husbands to find good jobs. He is a good man and would not have done this to Maria. You will not accuse him, Sheriff!'' Roberto was vehement.

"Roberto, someone did this to Maria, and logically, it was someone she knew well and liked. But I still don't understand why he was compelled to kill her. Why didn't he just arrange for an abortion?''

Roberto shook his head emphatically. "Maria would never have agreed to that. We are Catholic and believe abortions to be murder.''

"That strengthens my feeling that the murderer is a married man; otherwise he could have married Maria.''

"Maria did not want to get married, Sheriff, she wanted to go to college. I do not think even a baby would have forced her into marriage. My parents were very unhappy when she talked of college; they did not understand.''

Charles again felt compassion for the young girl. Pregnant, but not wanting to get married. Ambitious, but tied down with a baby. She must have been desperate. Desperate enough to try blackmail? He mulled the thought over. It would lend credulence to the motive. Sighing, he rose to his feet. "Roberto, I must ask these questions of your parents. Perhaps Maria told them more than you.''

"I think I must tell them, Sheriff. I could not explain your questions otherwise.''

Even after, when Charles thought about Maria Martinez, he would remember the small living room with its well-worn furniture, and the blank, suspicious faces of its occupants. Roberto's announcement of Maria's pregnancy was met with disbelief, then anger. Maria had been elevated to sainthood with her death. The real Maria, the young, ambitious, confused teenager, had never existed.

Roberto walked to the car with Charles and Raul. "I'm sorry, Sheriff, but they did not want to believe you. Maybe later they will talk, but not now. I will ask them again about men, but I do not think it will do any good. Right now, they would rather let her murderer go than admit she was not virtuous. They cannot stand it yet, Sheriff. Do you understand?"

"Yes, I understand. But the longer the murderer is free, the greater the chance he will never be caught. Right now, he is scared; he's liable to make mistakes during questioning. So I have to know if Maria ever told your parents anything."

"I will try, Sheriff."

Charles watched Roberto's lonely figure in the rearview mirror. "Dammit, Raul, why can't anything ever be simple? Why couldn't Maria be either a two-bit whore, or a saint, so I would know if I were looking for a man who couldn't resist temptation, or an out-and-out rapist? But no, she has to be a complex individual who is neither one nor the other. Hell, let's go talk to Leon McDaniels while we're out here. I presume he does live somewhere close."

"About a mile past the Martinez place, Sheriff. But I doubt he'll be at home," Raul answered.

"Why not?"

"He'll either be in the fields or in town at Frontier Days."

"Let's give him a try anyway. We haven't anything to lose."

Raul reversed the car, and they drove past the Martinez house again. Roberto was sitting on the front steps, his shoulders slumped in dejection. "I wonder if he's afraid to go back in the house?" Charles asked.

"Probably," said Raul. "He told the family something they didn't want to hear, and they're angry with him."

Raul approached a rambling ranch-style brick home surrounded by a beautifully landscaped yard. Isolated in the middle of the flat grain fields, with spruce trees and hedges softening the starkness, the house was typical of many of the newer farm homes. A peacock, his tail spread into a brilliant turquoise fan, set up a raucous cawing sound at the patrol car's approach. "Is that a peacock, or am I imagining things?"

"It's a peacock," replied Raul, driving up the wide circular drive with its evenly spaced hedge. "A lot of farmers keep them; they're as good as a watchdog any day of the week." Raul didn't realize how exotic the peacock seemed to Charles's urban eyes.

Charles knocked on the door and removed his hat as a neatly groomed woman in her forties opened the door. "Mrs. McDaniels?" he asked uncertainly. He didn't remember ever seeing Leon's wife before.

"Yes, Sheriff, I'm Geneva McDaniels. May I help you?" Her voice was soft, with none of the drawl Charles was accustomed to hearing.

"We need to talk to your husband. Maria Martinez was murdered, and your husband was present when the body was discovered. We're questioning everyone who was there."

"I knew poor Maria was murdered, of course, but I don't understand why you want to question my husband. He gave a statement or affidavit or something to your deputy. I don't think he has anything to add." The soft voice held a thread of steel.

"We'll need to ask some more questions, ma'am," Charles said. "Mr. McDaniels knew Maria for a long time, so he can be helpful in telling us something about her."

"I watched Maria Martinez grow up, too, Sheriff, and I'm not surprised she was killed. She probably brought it all on herself, playing up to all the men around here. Since my husband isn't here, I hope you'll excuse me; I have things to do."

Mrs. McDaniels started to close the door, but Charles grabbed the edge and held it open. For a moment he could see the woman was considering slamming it shut, and he braced himself.

"Mrs. McDaniels, I'll talk to your husband here or in my office. And I would like you to explain your statement about Maria."

Geneva McDaniels' lips compressed themselves into a

straight line. "My husband is in town at Frontier Days. You can find him there. As for myself, I have nothing further to say. If you want to arrest me, go ahead. I still have nothing to say." Her eyes were glittering with suppressed anger. Charles removed his hands from the door and it was immediately slammed shut.

"How interesting," he murmured.

# CHAPTER

# 9

"THIS IS CRAWFORD THIRTY-TWO, COME IN," Charles said, sliding down in the front seat and bracing his knees against the dashboard.

"Crawford thirty-two, where are you?" Mabel's nasal voice was unmistakable.

"We're on 1283 heading toward town. Are there any problems, Mabel?"

"We have a complaint about gambling at Frontier Days, Sheriff. Some of the ladies are very upset." Mabel's voice suggested that the sheriff probably knew all about it and was taking a cut of the proceeds.

"What kind of gambling?" Charles asked, gritting his teeth. He wondered which would go first, Mabel or his teeth.

"Bingo!" Mabel said.

"Mabel, listen very carefully. The bingo game is operated by the civic club that sponsors Frontier Days. It is a fair game, no one gets cheated, and the proceeds are donated to charity."

"But it's illegal, Sheriff!" Mabel squawked.

"Technically it is for the present. Now if those ladies want to go down to L.D.'s office and sign a complaint, then I will tell Jim Bob the Frontier Days' bingo game has to be closed down. I can't do it if they are not willing to sign their names on a formal complaint. Do you understand, Mabel?"

"Sheriff Johnson would have done something about it," Mabel said.

"Sheriff Johnson wouldn't have shut down the bingo game, Mabel, he ran the damn thing!" Charles shouted. "Now did anything else happen?"

"Meenie called in, Sheriff. He said he had found something."

"When did he call?" Charles asked, jerking upright with excitement.

"About an hour ago, Sheriff," she replied.

"Why the hell wasn't I told?" Charles yelled.

"You had your radio turned off," Mabel answered. Charles could almost see her smug expression.

"I told you to send a patrol car to get me if anything happened." Charles felt like committing murder himself.

"The patrol cars were all busy, Sheriff."

"For something important, Mabel, you call in an off-duty deputy."

"How was I to know this was important?" Mabel asked. "No one ever tells me anything."

"If Meenie tells you to get hold of me, it's important. Do you understand, Mabel?"

"Yes, Sheriff." The reply was subdued.

"Crawford thirty-two, ten-four," he said, and hung up the microphone.

"You didn't ask where Meenie was," Raul reminded him.

"He's on 1283 somewhere, probably fairly close. I told him to concentrate on the tailwater pits close to the scene of Billy Joe's murder. Let's just drive down the road. If we don't find him quickly, I'll swallow my pride and call Mabel."

Raul turned onto 1283 and Charles saw Meenie's patrol car in the distance. "There he is. I knew my luck had to turn."

"Things are looking better," Raul said. "We know how Maria felt about certain men, and we know something is rotten in the McDaniels's household."

"Oh, I'm not talking about the murder, I'm talking about not having to call Mabel back. The murder is worse than ever. Now we have a spiteful woman giving us still another view of Maria. Maria's got more facets than a diamond." Charles climbed out of the car.

"We found it, Sheriff," called Meenie, standing on top of the tailwater pit. Fifty feet wide and one hundred feet long, the pit was smaller than average. Used as a means of conserving irrigation water, tailwater pits were a common sight in the arid

Texas and Oklahoma Panhandles. They were dug at the lowest point of a field, so run-off water from row irrigation was caught and saved, then pumped back onto the crops. Water was literally more precious than oil in an area where the average rainfall might be only a dozen inches a year.

Charles and Meenie knelt down by the end of the embankment of the pit. A brownish smear stained the trampled weeds. Charles felt new respect for his deputy. A less careful person would have overlooked the few broken weeds and discoloration. Charles's eyes followed the minute splotches that made a crooked line to the edge of the asphalt. Meenie motioned him over to the road and pointed out stains on the asphalt itself to the point where they disappeared abruptly. "Probably threw her in a car or, more likely, a pickup bed," said Meenie, and carefully spat to one side.

He circled around the blood and led the sheriff back to the pit. "That guy just had bad luck all the way around, or Billy Joe had good luck. Come 'round to the back of the pit, Sheriff. Billy Joe or someone was sittin' by the irrigation pump drinkin' beer; there's still part of a six-pack left. Fingerprints will tell us if it was Billy Joe or not. He had his pickup parked back here, too; there's the tracks. That's why whoever it was didn't see him: his pickup was hidden, too."

"Why would Billy Joe come out here to drink beer?" Charles asked.

"Hell, who knows?" Meenie answered.

"Get out the evidence kit and pack and label everything. We still have to send it off to the lab. It would be embarrassing if it turned out to be animal blood of some kind."

"Where's the animal then, Sheriff?" Meenie shook his head. "You can count on it being human blood. If it's not Maria's, then we got another dead body we ain't found yet."

Charles had a macabre vision of dead bodies turning up in odd places all over the county. He shuddered. "I think two bodies are enough, Meenie. Get this stuff labeled and come on back to town." Charles stood a minute surveying the fields of sorghum and corn. "So Leon McDaniels owns all this."

Meenie shifted his tobacco and spat at a beetle crawling through the weeds. "Hell, no, Sheriff. Leon owns part of it,

L.D.'s daddy owns part of it, Jim Bob's got a couple of sections down the road a piece. This is the best farm land in the county, Sheriff; everybody's got a piece of it. The land north and south is too rough for farmin'; all the cattle raisin' is done there.''

"At least you didn't tell me our old friend Sammy owns a farm along here."

"Sure, he does, Sheriff. Any family that settled this region grabbed land in this section."

"So half the county would have a legitimate reason for being out on this road at night," Charles said.

"That's right. No one would possibly remember a pickup if they saw it," Meenie agreed.

"Our murderer certainly has good protective coloring. He can come out here late at night, and everyone would presume he had a good reason. By the way, Meenie, did you see any sign of what caused Maria's skull fracture?"

"Nope! Of course, I didn't know what I might be looking for, either."

"A big rock, a wrench, a hammer—the traditional blunt instrument."

"Ain't many loose rocks layin' around this part of the county, and I didn't see anything else either."

"How much water is in the tailwater pit, Meenie?" Charles asked, eyeing the dirt embankments.

"I'd guess maybe six or eight feet right now. I don't think Leon's irrigated for a couple of days."

"Meenie, I think you'd better look in the tailwater pit," Charles said.

Meenie pulled his hat off and threw it down, stomping the ground like a western Rumpelstiltskin.

"Holy hell, Sheriff, I can't swim, and I hate mud."

"I'll get hold of Leon and tell him we have to drain the tailwater pit. I never saw anyone with such an aversion to a little dirt."

"You ain't never known the Panhandle when a duster hit, or cowboyed down on the Canadian where you had to chase cows out in the muddy river bottom."

"I promise you, Meenie, no more muddy jobs for a while. Just find that weapon."

"If I get all muddy, it sure better be there," Meenie said ominously, as he replaced his hat and stomped away.

"Let's get going, Raul. I want to make a fast trip back to town and find Leon before Meenie decides to quit." Raul obligingly turned on the siren and made a fast turn that included squealing tires.

Charles braced his feet against the floorboard and prayed his seat-belt harness was really the safety measure it was supposed to be. As Raul took the last curve into town and the three-story brick courthouse came into view, Charles vowed never again to tell him to make it a fast trip. As the car swerved into a parking place in front of the courthouse, Charles let out the breath he hadn't even been conscious he was holding. Unbuckling his seat belt and climbing out on shaky legs, he glanced at his impassive deputy. "Did you ever want to drive race cars?"

Raul grinned. "You did say a fast trip, Sheriff."

"I'll try to remember not to make that mistake again. Go find Leon McDaniels in all that mess," Charles said, gesturing toward the food stands, carnival rides, and midway. "Tell him I also need to ask some questions about the Martinez family."

Charles reached in his pocket and pulled out a few crumpled bills. "Buy us some of those hamburgers Jim Bob's bunch makes. I've been waiting all year for those." Raul took the money and threaded his way through the crowd, while Charles climbed the courthouse steps.

Settled back at his desk, he called Slim in. "Where are the ladies who wanted the bingo game closed down?"

Slim scratched his head and grinned. "Well, Sheriff, they went on down to L.D. Lassiter's office to sign a complaint, but L.D., he didn't want to take it, so he climbed out his office window and snuck up the back stairs. He's been hidin' out in the court reporter's office for the last couple hours."

Charles leaned his head back and laughed. His face lost its sternness and looked boyish and appealing. He didn't know his deputy was watching in amazement, wondering why the sheriff didn't laugh more often.

\* \* \*

From a distance, Leon McDaniels looked like a middle-aged Viking, with his blond hair graying at the temples, bright blue eyes, and the red-brown color that blonds so often turn in the sun. An attractive man, Charles thought, but surely, to Maria's young eyes, an old man.

"Mr. McDaniels, a few questions." Charles leaned forward, folding his hands on his desk. "Mr. McDaniels, we have reason to believe that Maria Martinez was murdered on your property. We found blood by your tailwater pit on 1283. We'd like your permission to drain the pit so we can look for the murder weapon."

"What was it, Sheriff?" McDaniels asked, cracking his knuckles, his face troubled.

"I don't know. I don't even know if it's in the pit, but we have to look."

"Go ahead; anything to help. Poor little Maria," he murmured, looking down at his hands.

Charles stepped to the door of his office. "Mabel, get Meenie on the radio and tell him to drain the pit."

"Yes, Sheriff," she said, then hesitated. "The ladies from the church are still waiting for Mr. Lassiter."

"What ladies and what church?" Charles asked, his mind on the upcoming interview with Leon McDaniels.

Mabel named a small fundamentalist church Charles had never heard of: The Temple of the Redeemed Souls. "You remember, Sheriff, the ladies with the complaint about the bingo. They believe it's corrupting our youth."

"There's a lot of things corrupting our youth, Mabel, but I don't think their immortal souls are in danger from bingo. As I told you before, I have to have a signed and filed complaint in order to close down the game. As for Mr. Lassiter, I'm sure he's somewhere. Perhaps they should go on home and try again tomorrow." Charles's patience was wearing thin.

"They feel awful strong about this, Sheriff," said Mabel, her voice holding a hint of warning.

"They'll just have to wait until L.D. shows up to take their complaint, Mabel." Charles closed the door and grabbed one of the hamburgers. "If you knew how I looked forward to these each year. The man who could duplicate these in a fast-food chain would make a million dollars overnight." He bit into it and found it just as good as he remembered: hot and peppery, one hundred percent beef, with mustard and bun.

Putting his cup down and throwing the grease-splattered paper napkin from the hamburger in the general direction of the trash can, Charles nodded imperceptibly at Raul. Waiting until he saw the deputy pull out his notebook and pen, he cleared his throat and began.

"Mr. McDaniels, I need to ask you some questions about your actions on Saturday night. According to what you wrote down the other day when her body was discovered, you were out checking the irrigation water in your fields until around twelve o'clock. You then went home. Do you have any witnesses who can support that statement?"

"Why should I need witnesses? Why are you checking my movements?"

"You knew Maria; you knew the barbecue pit was dug a day early; and you have no alibi for the time of the murder."

"A lot of people knew Maria, and also knew about the barbecue pit! Probably half the county would have trouble with an alibi. Why am I being singled out?"

"You can also pilot a spray plane," Charles said.

"What does that have to do with Maria's murder?" Leon's indignation was giving way to puzzlement.

"Billy Joe Williams was murdered, and I believe his murder is tied to Maria's. Someone dumped a load of parathion on Billy Joe's pickup, then suffocated him."

"My God! That's a complicated way to kill someone. Why not just shoot him?"

"Because I think the killer hoped it would pass for an accidental death. It was just bad luck that it didn't."

"You still haven't explained why you think I would kill Maria, Sheriff. Unless you are planning to accuse everyone at the barbecue pit."

"I'm not accusing anyone," Charles said. The word "yet" was unspoken, but clearly understood.

"You still haven't answered my question. Why would I or anyone else want to kill Maria?"

"Maria was pregnant," Charles said bluntly.

"No, you're mistaken!" Leon cried. "Not my little Maria!" He grasped the edge of the desk, his ruddy face losing its color.

Charles kept his face expressionless. It was at this point that a suspect said more than he intended to. Shock would loosen his inhibitions. He watched Leon McDaniels disintegrate into a grieving man.

"The autopsy showed Maria to be pregnant," Charles repeated.

"She was so young, so beautiful, so alive. I had such plans for her. She was going to college; she was going to stay with my sister in Canyon. Pregnancy would have ruined all that!"

"You seem to be more upset about Maria's being pregnant than you are about her death. Why is that, Mr. McDaniels?" Charles asked, rising to lean over the desk, his hands braced on its surface.

"Maria wouldn't have slept with anyone. She wouldn't do that to me." McDaniels rocked back and forth, shaking his head.

"What do you have to do with it, Mr. McDaniels?" Charles asked. "You weren't her father, or even a member of her family. Why would she not do that to you? Do what, Mr. McDaniels? Be unfaithful?" Leon McDaniels didn't answer. He sat staring at his large, rough hands.

Charles leaned closer, his brown eyes relentless. "Did you kill her because she had slept with another man, or was it because she threatened to tell your wife if you didn't support her?"

"My God, Sheriff! If the baby had been mine, I would have married her! I loved her. Don't you understand? I loved her!"

Charles was stunned. He heard a half-uttered exclamation from Raul but ignored it. All his attention was focused on the man in front of him. He recoiled when McDaniels finally looked up. No one had the right to see inside another man's tortured soul.

"Who killed her, Sheriff?" His eyes were beseeching. He was a man who wanted to hear every detail from a personal tragedy, as if knowing the details would alleviate his suffering.

"Men kill for love, Leon. Are you one of them?" Charles asked softly.

"Was this a crime of love, Sheriff? Would a man who loved a woman allow her to be burned like trash? This was a crime of hate. Someone who is filled with hate did this." He looked up again at Charles, his eyes void of hope.

"I'm going home, Sheriff, I'll be there if you need me again." He rose, not waiting for permission, suddenly looking his age and more.

Charles wondered if he had just let a murderer walk out.

# CHAPTER

# 10

"SHERIFF!" SLIM'S VOICE DISTURBED CHARLES.

"What is it?" Charles wondered if it were possible to have one uninterrupted moment to think.

"Those ladies are picketing the bingo game! Jim Bob Brown is dancing around like he was stepping over cow manure and screaming to high heaven for you to arrest them. You better hurry. He's fixing to have a stroke."

"Oh, my God!" Charles groaned. For a few seconds he wondered if there was room in the court reporter's office for another public official to hide. "All right, I'm coming." Grabbing his hat and setting it firmly on his head, he strode into the outer office and stopped in front of the dispatcher's desk.

"Mabel, listen very carefully and repeat after me. I will call in all the men on patrol." Charles stopped.

Mabel looked at him, her mouth gaping open.

"I'm waiting, Mabel."

"I will call in all the men on patrol," she parroted.

"Very good!" Charles exclaimed. "I will call in all the off-duty deputies. Repeat that, please."

"I will call in all the off-duty deputies," she obediently said, her eyes staring at the sheriff as if he had suddenly sprouted horns.

"Good! You've repeated my instructions perfectly. Now do you suppose you can follow them this time?"

"Yes, sir," she said, her eyes round.

"Then you see that you do," Charles said firmly.

He headed for the elevator with Slim trailing along. "Remember, Slim, the secret of crowd control is to keep calm, isolate the troublemakers, and let them yell themselves out, and, for God's sake, don't get hit by a picket sign.''

Charles stepped off the elevator and headed toward the door. He could already hear the ladies singing, ''Bringing in the Sheaves.'' Above that he could hear Jim Bob screaming. Slim was right: Jim Bob was in imminent danger of a stroke. As he opened the courthouse door, the full effect of the scene hit him.

A small group of women carrying hand-lettered signs were marching around and around the open-sided booth that housed the bingo game. Seated on the benches that lined three sides of the booth were people of all ages and both sexes, clutching their bingo cards like good-luck tokens to ward off the evil eye. Inside the booth, sporting a rapidly swelling eye, stood Jim Bob Brown.

''Sheriff!'' he screamed, shaking his fist in the air. ''Do your duty! Arrest these fanatics!''

''Jim Bob, let's go inside the courthouse and talk about this.'' Charles walked over to the line of ladies. ''Excuse me, ladies,'' he said. The women continued marching, waving their signs and changing hymns. The rhythm of ''The Old Rugged Cross'' rang out over the courthouse lawn. Spectators were gathered four deep, and an enterprising man walked among the crowd selling Cokes and popcorn.

''Who is your spokeswoman?'' Charles asked loudly. He felt the sweat begin to trickle down his back. This wasn't going to be as easy as he hoped.

''It's that dame with the knot on top of her head, Sheriff,'' Jim Bob said, his face almost as red as the stitching on his shirt. ''Leastways, she's the one that walked up and announced that she was closing down the bingo game. Lock them up!''

''I think it's better to try to calm these ladies down than to lock them up. Just imagine what the television stations in Amarillo would make of that. You don't want your civic club held responsible for throwing old ladies in jail in violation of their civil rights.''

''What about *my* civil rights?'' Jim Bob squawked. ''Do you see this eye? Do you? Well, I didn't hit it on no doorknob. I was out there tryin' to talk to that old bat, and she just walked right over me; knocked me flat on my can. What in the hell am I supposed to do, Sheriff?''

Charles looked at the perspiring chairman for a moment. "How badly would your total profit be lowered if you donated, say, five percent of the bingo games to a worthy charity?''

"Net or gross profit, Sheriff?'' Jim Bob asked. Harvard Business School didn't have anything to teach Jim Bob about running this affair. "And what charity are you talking about anyway? This money's already earmarked.''

"Why don't you ask the, ah, lady with the topknot if her church doesn't need some new hymnals, or a stained-glass window, or new toys for the nursery. It's called bribery, Jim Bob.''

"If we let one group blackmail us, then everybody will try it. I refuse to be blackmailed!'' Jim Bob said indignantly.

"If you can survive this year, you're in good shape. There's a proposed amendment to the constitution to allow bingo games for charitable purposes, and I think we can all count on its passing. But for now, you just have to do the best you can. I suggest you try a little imagination, too.'' Charles fell silent to watch Jim Bob mull over his suggestion. Finally Jim Bob capitulated, nodding his head.

"I would still rather lock the old biddies up, but I can see where the TV people might not understand. And I wonder if these people are in the pay of the Rotarians. You ask them that, Sheriff; find out how many are married to Rotarians.'' Jim Bob viewed Rotarians as McCarthy had viewed Communists.

"Jim Bob, I don't want to hear anything about the Rotarians. They have better things to do with their money than to pay fanatics to march around carrying sings. Let's see if we can get those ladies to cooperate.''

"Good luck, Sheriff,'' Jim Bob said. "That old woman wouldn't listen if God himself spoke to her from a burning bush. She'd just grab a fire extinguisher and squirt it right in his eyes.''

"Jim Bob, you've got to use the right technique. Come on, Slim; let's talk to the ladies.'' Charles walked closer to the marching women.

"Don't say I didn't warn you, Sheriff,'' Jim Bob called.

"Ladies, Jim Bob Brown and I would like to talk to you about the bingo game. I think it's always better to talk about disagreements than to fight about them, don't you?" Charles's voice was loud, but he might as well have whispered for all the attention he received. Charles tried again, his voice audible over the hymn.

"Ladies, I'm asking you nicely to come inside to talk to Jim Bob or anybody else from the Frontier Days committee about your complaint." Charles waited, but could see no indication the women intended to talk to anyone. They had to have a weak point; it was just a matter of finding it. He looked speculatively at the uniformly neat, lacquered hair of the women. Maybe there was a way. He motioned to Raul and Jim Bob.

"Raul, take some deputies and move the crowd off the lawn. Jim Bob, go ask the people around the bingo game to take their cards and move out of the booth and onto the sidewalk."

"What are you going to do, Sheriff?" Jim Bob asked.

"I told you that you just had to use the right technique, and I've found it. When I'm finished, they may be willing to make a dignified retreat to the courthouse."

Jim Bob walked to the booth, staying well away from the marching women, and began to whisper to the bingo players. Reluctantly they moved, carrying their cards with them, throwing, distrustful looks at the sheriff and Jim Bob. Bingo players take the game seriously.

Charles walked to the side of the courthouse and waited until the crowds were clear of the lawn. Several of the marching women glanced around nervously, but the sudden isolation affected neither their volume nor their determination. Charles crossed his fingers and turned on the sprinklers. For a second nothing happened, then geysers of spray erupted from the ground. The chorus of "Rock of Ages" turned into squeals as the women frantically shifted their signs in an attempt to protect their elaborate hairdos. In a matter of seconds, lacquered curls turned into soppy tangles. By ones and twos, signs were dropped and women scurried for the shelter of the courthouse porch, until only the leader of the group remained. Charles felt a flicker of admiration as she put her sign over her shoulder and walked to the courthouse, dignity intact.

Jim Bob grinned and slapped Charles on the back. "I knew there was a good reason for voting for you, Sheriff."

Charles turned off the sprinklers and walked up to the bedraggled group of women. "Ladies, I think Jim Bob Brown would like to meet with you to discuss your differences."

The leader, whose gray hair was worn in an uncompromising knot at the back of her head, looked at the sheriff, a twinkle in her blue eyes. "Sheriff, I have to hand it to you: you certainly know what a lady's priorities are. You have a lot of gumption, young man. Now, shall we get down to business? I presume you've talked that loudmouth Jim Bob Brown into making some kind of proposition. Let's hear it. Your little trick with the sprinkler probably lost me three-fourths of my support. I need to get what I can out of it. Quit staring at me like a fish out of water, and let's get to talking."

"Yes, ma'am," Charles said, feeling very sure that any further confrontation with this woman might very well end with his coming off second best. He ushered the ladies into the courthouse. "I think we had better go up to the courtroom; my office is a little small." He gestured for Jim Bob to follow.

"That will be satisfactory, Sheriff. I trust this won't take long. I think we all need to change into dry clothes."

"And I need to call the beauty shop," one of the women said.

"Hattie, vanity is one of the seven deadly sins," snapped the leader. "You would do well to remember that."

Charles cleared his throat, hoping he could get through the meeting without laughing. "I'm Sheriff Matthews. I don't believe I've ever met you."

"I'm Miss Megan Elizabeth Poole, Sheriff. I organized this little demonstration. Ladies," she said, turning to face her followers. "We'll take the stairs. Exercise is good for women our age." She glared at the few who hesitated.

Charles grinned at Jim Bob. "After you," he said, realizing he was thoroughly enjoying himself. Jim Bob rolled his eyes, but resolutely began climbing.

"Were you a teacher, Miss Poole?" Charles asked.

"For thirty-five years, young man," she answered.

"I thought so. You have a certain air of authority."

"Are you being facetious, young man?"

"No, ma'am. You just remind me of my fifth-grade teacher."

"Were you fond of her?"

"No, but I respected her," Charles answered.

"Good! That's as it should be."

Miss Poole marched into the courtroom and pointed to the first row of seats. "Take your places, ladies, and we'll listen to what Mr. Brown has to say." She took the end seat and looked expectantly at Jim Bob. "Well, Jim Bob, don't just stand there with your mouth open. What do you have to say for yourself. Speak up!"

Jim Bob blushed. Charles was amazed at the sight of a dark pink color flooding Jim Bob's naturally ruddy cheeks. He would never have thought to see Jim Bob Brown reduced to the status of a gibbering schoolboy.

"Well?" said Miss Poole firmly.

"Miss Poole, ma'am," Jim Bob said. "You know the bingo game is a popular booth. It's run fairly. It brings in a lot of money for charity. If we have to close it down, there'll be a lot of kids who need help that won't get it. You don't really believe it's sinful, do you?" he asked hopefully.

"It's against the law, Jim Bob," Miss Poole said. "I don't believe you can excuse it by saying the proceeds go to charity."

"Excuse me, Jim Bob," Charles said, enjoying himself hugely. "Miss Poole, staging a demonstration without a license is also against the law."

Miss Poole looked uncomfortable for a moment. "You're right, young man. And two wrongs don't make a right."

"Miss Poole, bingo is a good, clean game that costs very little and does benefit a lot of people. You do agree this is a God-fearing community, don't you?" Charles asked suddenly.

"Yes," she said, her eyes narrowing as she tried to anticipate what point this smooth-talking young man was trying to make.

"God handed down no edict against bingo, Miss Poole. And

sometimes we interpret man-made laws according to community standards. This community doesn't feel the bingo game at Frontier Days to be gambling. I trust the people in Crawford County and I respect their judgment. Therefore, I would rather not close down the game. If you are concerned about the proceeds or worried about whether it is operated honestly, I suggest you volunteer to help Jim Bob in some capacity. Perhaps he could use your help in calling numbers or handing out the prizes." Charles ignored the sputtering sounds from Jim Bob.

"I hadn't considered those points, Sheriff. I was, perhaps, reading more into God's word than he intended."

"I believe it's a common failing, Miss Poole," Charles said.

"The ladies and I will volunteer to help run the booth. Jim Bob, you may call me later with the schedule. Ladies, you may rise."

Miss Poole marched majestically out, her entourage of wet hens following.

Jim Bob stared at the courtroom doors as they closed softly behind the departing ladies. "Dammit to hell, Sheriff, do you know what you've done? I'll have that old battle-ax trying to run the whole celebration. My God, I'd rather have my mother-in-law in that booth!"

"It's better than my having to close you down. And L.D. can't stay hidden in the court reporter's office forever. This way, you have your bingo, and I don't have to lock up a bunch of nice old ladies."

"Nice! Nice, did you say?" he sputtered. "If you think that old piranha is nice, you'd just love my mother-in-law. I'm going back out and draw up a schedule. A schedule, for God's sake!"

"Jim Bob, before you leave, I need to talk to you in my office."

"Talk to me! Just look where your talkin' landed me. I don't want to talk to you!"

"Jim Bob, it's not a matter of choice." Charles felt almost guilty about questioning Jim Bob. In some unidentified way, he found the man more likable. Perhaps it was the blush when

Miss Poole chastised him. Charles found it difficult to conceive of a murderer who could blush.

"What do you mean, Sheriff?" Jim Bob asked, his expression both puzzled and guarded.

"I have some more questions about the murder," Charles said, striding through the big double doors of the courtroom and on into the Sheriff's Department.

"I told you all I knew yesterday, Sheriff." Jim Bob stopped at the door to Charles's office.

The sheriff gently herded him through the door. "Jim Bob, some other things have been discovered since yesterday."

Jim Bob sat down heavily in one of the wooden armchairs and took off his hat. His white shirt looked dingy, its crispness a victim of the hot August sun. "God, I'm tired. First that body yesterday. Then we had to throw away nearly three tons of meat. Now, this psalm-singing fanatic today. What else can happen?" He threw his hands out in a dramatic gesture.

Charles raised his voice. "Raul, come on in." He waited a moment until the deputy had closed the door. Sighing, he looked around the room with its institutional green walls, brown tile floor, and pre–World War II furnishings. It looked nothing like his office in Dallas, but it too had been a silent witness to countless sessions like this one. Its wood and plaster were permeated with the fear and guilt of a thousand cases.

Charles blinked his eyes to close out the past and studied Jim Bob. Standing over six feet, Jim Bob Brown was barrel-chested and slightly overweight, or, in the Panhandle vernacular, hefty. Blond hair, blue eyes, ruddy complexion, the epitome of the predominantly Anglo settlers of the area. One of the first things Charles had noticed about Crawford County was its brown and white coloration. Everyone seemed to have blond hair, blue eyes, and fair skin, or black hair, brown eyes, and olive skin. Intermarriage between Mexican-Americans and Anglos was relatively uncommon in the region, so the races had not blended to any great degree to develop a variety of shades of skin.

"Well, Sheriff, what do you want to know? I haven't got all day; I've got to make out a schedule for that damn old woman." Jim Bob was still rankled.

"Jim Bob, the body in the pit was Maria Martinez."

"Maria! Oh, my God!" Jim Bob exclaimed.

"She was pregnant," Charles added, brown eyes focused on Jim Bob, looking for any reaction.

"Maria was pregnant! Well, Sheriff, all you got to do is find the father."

"It's a little more complicated, Jim Bob. Apparently Billy Joe Williams witnessed the murder and tried a little blackmail. He, too, was murdered. The murderer used a spray plane."

"A spray plane!" Jim Bob exclaimed. "What in hell did he do? Land on him?" He slapped his knee and doubled over with laughter.

"No, he dumped a load of parathion on him and then strangled him, and Jim Bob, I don't find it one bit funny," Charles snapped, disgusted with the big man's crude remarks.

Jim Bob sobered, looking ashamed. "I'm sorry, Sheriff. I know it's not funny, but that's a dumb way to kill a man."

"It might have been written off as an accident if Billy Joe hadn't bruised quite so easily."

"What's all that got to do with me?" Jim Bob pulled out a bandana and wiped his face.

"You knew Maria, you can fly a spray plane, and you have no alibi for Saturday."

"Everybody in town knew Maria, and a lot of folks can pilot a spray plane. Why are you picking on me?"

"You knew about the barbecue pit being dug a day early, and you have no alibi. Where were you Saturday night?"

"That's none of your business, Sheriff. There are other people involved, and I won't give their names."

"Jim Bob, it is my business. Maria talked a lot about you. She liked you. Just how well did she like you? Well enough to let you make love to her?"

Jim Bob flushed, and his eyes darted away to focus on the corner of the room. "I didn't kill her. She was a nice girl. She gave everybody the come-on, but I didn't take advantage of her."

"Did you make love to her? Did she try to blackmail you when she found out she was pregnant? Did she threaten to tell your wife?"

"I'm not going to answer your questions. I didn't kill her, and you can't prove I did!" Jim Bob shouted.

"That kind of attitude is not going to help you. I'll ask you again. Where were you on Saturday night, Jim Bob?"

"And I'll tell you again, I'm not going to answer your questions, Sheriff. I'm not under arrest, and I don't have to sit here and listen to you. I'm leaving." Jim Bob grabbed his hat and jammed it on his head.

"Your refusal to answer my questions puts you in a very awkward position. We aren't totally without physical evidence. Brace yourself, Jim Bob, because I'm going to investigate you thoroughly. I'll find out where you were Saturday night, and I'll remember how uncooperative you were. If you didn't kill that girl, you're acting very callously toward hearing about her death."

"Sheriff, I'm sorry she's dead. I liked her a lot. I'm not being callous; I just can't feel much right now. And nobody's ever called me a murderer before."

"I'm not calling you a murderer, Jim Bob, I'm questioning everybody who fits the criteria and has no alibi. I want to mark you off my list of suspects, but I can't unless you tell me the truth. What is it going to be? I can investigate and dig up all the old secrets you'd rather be forgotten, or you can tell me where you were Saturday." Charles folded his arms across his chest and watched Jim Bob.

"I can't tell you, Sheriff. But I didn't kill her. How can anyone kill something so pretty, and small, and soft?"

"Someone could, Jim Bob," the sheriff answered.

# CHAPTER

# 11

"DAMN, RAUL, I DON'T HAVE ENOUGH HARD EVI-
dence to even go to the judge to ask for a warrant to check the
tires on his car. Jim Bob can refuse to answer any questions
until hell freezes over, and there's not a thing I can do about it.
He was doing something Saturday he doesn't want us to know
about, but I don't think it was killing Maria. If he had killed
her, he would have a gold-plated alibi. But I can't eliminate
him until I know where he was. Do you think he was sleeping
with her?" Charles asked, crossing his legs on top of the desk.

"I don't know if he actually was or was just dreaming about
it, Sheriff, but he's acting guilty about something.

"And then there's Leon. Dammit, I can't see him committing a deliberate murder. Oh, I could see his becoming angry
at Maria and striking her, then trying to hide the body. But I
can't see his killing Billy Joe." Charles ran his fingers through
his hair, his own unconscious gesture of frustration.

"You can't see him as a murderer, or you won't see him?"
Raul asked softly.

Charles dropped his hands and looked at his deputy. "Are
you suggesting that I'm letting personalities interfere with my
judgment?" His voice was low and expressionless. Only a
close friend could recognize the anger.

The door burst open and Meenie stomped in, his uniform
caked with mud. Dropping a plastic evidence bag on the desk,
he spat belligerently, but accurately, in the sheriff's spittoon.

"If that ain't your murder weapon, Sheriff, then that's too
bad. That wrench is the only thing we found besides empty
beer cans. It's so covered with mud, I don't think the lab is
going to be able to find a thing on it one way or the other. I just

want you to know I ain't gonna wade in any more mud holes. A man's got his limits."

"I promise, Meenie, no more mud. Bundle it up and send it to the Department of Public Safety lab in Austin with a request to rush it through."

Meenie rolled his eyes toward the ceiling. "Rush it through, the man says. Hell, we'll be lucky if the suspects don't die of old age before that lab gets around to sendin' us a report."

"Send it in anyway; we don't have much choice. And thanks, Meenie." Charles grinned at his mud-splattered deputy.

"Oh, think nothing of it, Sheriff. You just stand around in hundred-degree heat waiting for a tailwater pit to drain. Then you take your boots off and roll your pants legs up and tramp around in mud past your ankles. Like I said, a man's got his limits, and I'm way past mine." Meenie picked up the evidence bag and stomped out of the office.

"All right, Raul, you heard him. Next mud detail goes to you. Equal opportunity, and all that."

"What about you, Sheriff?" Raul asked, a wide smile stretching his mouth.

"Rank has its privileges. One of those privileges is assigning the dirty work, or I should say muddy work, to my subordinates."

Charles laced his hands together behind his head and leaned back in his chair. "Speaking of rank, has anyone told L.D. he can come out of hiding?"

"No, I don't think so."

"L.D. is a damn slick politician, Raul. Want to bet he could have managed to stay out of sight until Saturday, when Frontier Days are over?"

"I won't bet with you on L.D. He's a very smart man. But you solved the problem, Sheriff, and you didn't have to hide or throw anyone in jail. That makes you very smart, too."

"I'm so smart that I've got a killer loose and I don't know how to catch him. I can't get a warrant to check Jim Bob's or Leon's tires because I don't really have probable cause, just a half-baked idea about the murderer having to meet certain criteria. I don't have any hard evidence of anything. All I have are suspects, and not very many of those." Charles dropped his feet to the floor and stood up to pace the room in agitation. "I don't know. I just don't know."

"Something will break, Sheriff. The murderer will make a mistake," Raul said, a little shaken by the Sheriff's depression.

"Not this one, Raul. I prosecuted a lot of murder cases when I was in Dallas, and I never saw a case with so few physical clues to the killer's identity. As for the criteria I'm so proud of, it means nothing. The law will not allow me to badger someone without just cause. A good attorney, or even a bad one, will pin my ears to the wall on my so-called criteria merely by pointing out how many men in this county they could fit. No, I can't haul those men in for endless rounds of questioning without more evidence. I need another witness."

Charles pounded a fist against the palm of his hand. "Damn, Raul, every time a man gets drunk, steps out on his wife, buys a car, or makes a fool of himself, everyone in town knows about it. How in the hell can a man get Maria pregnant, kill her, and dump her in the barbecue pit, with no one the wiser?"

"Sheriff!" Slim struck his freckled face inside the door. "What are we going to do with Old Ben? He threw his breakfast on the floor; claims we're trying to poison him."

"All right, Slim, I'll go talk to him. If he's not sick, I'm going to let him out. You weren't planning on pressing charges, were you?" Charles asked, walking to the door.

"Hell, no, Sheriff. He's just an old man. A strong old man," Slim added, touching a discernibly purple bruise on his chin.

Charles passed by the dispatcher's desk to the steel door that led to the jail cells. He slapped his pockets to make sure he wasn't carrying anything that could conceivably be used for a weapon. The aisle between the cells was so narrow it was possible for a prisoner to reach anyone walking down the center of it.

Charles motioned for Claude Evans, the jailer, to unlock the door. "Go back to the office; I'll talk to him alone."

"I ain't supposed to do that, Sheriff; no one is to be alone in the jail without a backup man in case of an emergency. You never know when one of these prisoners will go berserk and try to start a riot. Be real embarrassing if they held the sheriff hostage." Evans slapped his leg and laughed heartily.

Charles felt a moment's irritation; he was the one who had formulated that rule after Slim had been tied to the bars with his own belt by a grizzled young man serving ninety days on a drunk and disorderly charge. "Then go wait at the end of the cell block. I don't think Old Ben is going to assault me."

Not wanting to see the jailer's reaction to his words, Charles closed the cell door and sat down on the hard bunk. He put his hand on Old Ben's arm and was startled when the man screamed and skittered over to the corner of the cell.

"Ben, it's me, Sheriff Matthews. It's all right; no one is going to hurt you." He saw awareness creep over the man's face and his shoulders lose their rigidity. Walking sideways like a crab, Ben edged back over to the bunk, his eyes darting from side to side.

Charles patted the bunk. "Sit down, Ben, and talk to me."

"No!" The old man sat hugging himself, rocking back and forth, not looking at the sheriff. "No," he repeated.

"I can't keep you locked up. Slim isn't going to press charges, and the jail isn't a hotel," Charles said gently.

Old Ben wiped his nose on the white denim jail uniform. "You don't understand, Sheriff."

"What don't I understand, Ben?"

The old man shook his head, swinging it from left to right like a stunned bull. "I don't know."

Charles raked his fingers through his hair in frustration. Damn stubborn old man anyway. "Ben, I'm letting you out tomorrow unless you give me some reason why I shouldn't. Can you do that, Ben? Can you give me a reason?" He heard the pleading in his voice and hoped the old man would respond.

Old Ben looked up, hopeless resignation in his faded blue eyes. "I am a coward."

"Why are you a coward? Tell me."

"Leave me alone, Sheriff. I won't bother anybody anymore." Old Ben folded his hands and looked down at the floor, withdrawing into himself.

Charles touched his shoulder but didn't think Old Ben was even aware of him. Feeling frustrated, he motioned to the jailer to unlock the cell door. The silence behind him was broken only by the strenuous breathing of Old Ben.

"You ready to be sprung, Sheriff?" Evans asked. "I tell you what: there's a lot worse jails in the country than Crawford County Jail. Ain't that right, Old Ben?" The jailer stared perplexedly at the old man. "Now what's got into him, Sheriff? He's usually real friendly."

Charles turned back to look through the bars at Old Ben. The old man never looked up, continuing to study the rough texture of the cement floor. Charles shook his head; he had done all he could. The old man would have to make up his mind whether he wanted help or not.

"Goodbye, Ben." He waited, but the old man refused to answer or even to give any indication he had heard.

Charles returned to his office, feeling he had failed the old man, but knowing also there was nothing he could do. He closed his eyes and felt the grit of sleeplessness. Technically he could go home, but there were too many problems. Now there was the additional problem of Old Ben. He answered the knock on his door without looking up.

"Come in," he said wearily.

L.D. stuck his head inside the office, a sheepish grin on his face. "I take it the fireworks are over, and I can come out of hiding."

Charles looked up at his friend, a tired smile lightening the corners of his mouth. "You coward, leaving that mess on my shoulders."

"Look at it this way: you needed some experience in dealing with little old ladies. Besides, you didn't have Miss Poole in the sixth grade; you didn't begin the confrontation already feeling intimidated."

"She was your sixth-grade teacher?"

L.D. sank into a chair and hooked one leg over the arm. "Everyone had Miss Poole in the sixth grade. Death, taxes, and Miss Poole are three facts of life in Carroll. I hated the old lady, and the feeling was mutual. I don't feel guilty about hiding out. I planned to lock myself up in jail if necessary."

"Speaking of jail I have Old Ben locked up," Charles began.

"It's not the end of the month," L.D. said. "What's he doing in jail?"

"Technically, he assaulted a sheriff's deputy," Charles said, and held up his hand at L.D. "Wait, that's not all. He's sitting in his cell claiming we're trying to poison him and saying he's a coward. I think he's afraid of something, but he won't tell me anything. Slim isn't going to press charges, so I have to release the old man. But I don't want to. I swear he's scared to death, and I feel responsible for him."

"It sounds like he needs to be committed to the mental health facility in Amarillo for observation. I've dealt with a lot of alcoholics, and most of them end up paranoid. Let me talk to him. If I think he's mentally incapacitated, then I'll round up two doctors to examine him."

"Do you know anything about him, L.D.? Do you know anything about his past that might explain what's wrong with him?"

"Charles, he's just an old drunk. That's all he's ever been. You can't play nursemaid to everybody in the county. Develop some objectivity, or you're going to have a breakdown. You look like hell."

Charles rubbed his hand over his face. "All right, L.D., talk to him and make your observations. I have to do something with him tomorrow; I can't keep him any longer without charging him with something. And you're right, I am trying to be a nursemaid."

L.D. pushed himself to his feet and smoothed at his blond hair. "Okay, I'll go talk to him." He paused at the door. "Angie wants to know if you're coming to dinner. She thinks you don't eat unless she feeds you."

Charles grinned, his mask dropping momentarily to reveal his affection for his friend. "I can't tonight, L.D. There's still a witness I want to talk to. Tell Angie I'll call if I can make it tomorrow. And L.D., thanks."

"I'll drop by after I talk to Ben. Maybe you'll change your

mind about that meal." L.D. closed the door, and Charles picked up the pile of statements taken at the barbecue pit.

Somewhere there had to be a clue.

Charles walked across the courthouse lawn, absorbing the sight, smell, and noise of Frontier Days. He wished he could walk around and talk to the people he knew, watch the young children taking their first ride on the merry-go-round, and just relax. But murder wasn't conducive to relaxation. Neither was being harangued by Mrs. Cora Jenkins who claimed Sammy Phillips had fondled her young daughter. Threading his way through the crowds of teenage couples clustered around the carnival rides, Charles approached the dunking tank. He could see the line of boys in western shirts flexing their muscles, pubescent males looking for a date. Good-natured banter bounced back and forth between the boys and the bikini-clad girl currently on the board.

He stood back and watched the short figure of Sammy as he collected money and passed out baseballs. Charles waited patiently until a tall, muscular teenager hit the bull's eye to spill the lissome young girl into the round, corrugated-tin stock tank that served as the dunking pool. His eyes narrowed as he watched Sammy's fat figure rush to the tank. Although he doubted the girl needed any help in getting out of the water, Charles could detect no impropriety in Sammy's actions. He was merely taking advantage of the opportunity to touch young girls in a socially acceptable manner. He walked up and tapped Sammy's shoulder.

"Get someone to fill in. I need to talk to you a minute."

The shorter man turned around, piggish eyes narrowing. "Hell, Sheriff, if it's about that Jenkins girl, I didn't do nothing."

"I had to listen to her story, now I want to hear your side. Come on up to the office, Sammy, and let's talk about it." Charles walked away, only to turn back when Sammy didn't follow.

"Sammy, I don't think you want me to question you in front of everybody, but it's up to you. I can do it here where everybody can overhear if they try, or we can go to my office."

Sammy motioned to another man clad in an identical white western shirt and turned over his money box. "Frank, take over for me. The sheriff needs some help."

Sammy swaggered over to Charles, a smirk on his face. "All right, Sheriff, let's get this over with. I got better things to do than to talk to you."

Charles felt his usual disgust and dislike rise to lodge in his throat like an indigestible piece of meat. Unconsciously he clenched one hand into a fist, then forced himself to relax. He wished Sammy were guilty of fondling that girl; he would like nothing better than to lock up this lump of suet.

"I think you might find it a good idea to talk to me, Sammy, and not just about the Jenkins girl. And I also suggest you sweeten your tone just a little bit before I get mad. I can be a real bastard when I'm mad." Charles stared into Sammy's piglike eyes.

Neither man spoke as they wound their way through the crowd and up to Charles's office. Their antipathy for one another was too great to mask with small talk. A few curious eyes followed their progress, but there were too many distractions for anyone to indulge in idle speculation as to why two sworn enemies were walking together.

Charles took off his Stetson and placed it on the filing cabinet in the corner of his office. He leaned against his desk and crossed his arms, consciously choosing to exploit the intimidating advantage his height gave him. "Sit down, Sammy, and tell me your story about the Jenkins girl."

Sammy sat down in the chair farthest from the sheriff and pulled a cigar out of his pocket. Wetting the length of it with his tongue, he lit the end. Blowing out a cloud of aromatic smoke, he leered at Charles. "There ain't nothin' to tell, Sheriff. The little girl slipped on the edge of the tank. It ain't my fault if I hit her boob when I caught her. Hell, if I'm goin' to cop a feel, I'll pick someone with something upstairs. That Jenkins girl ain't got no more than two peas on a board. And I sure wouldn't have done nothing with that witch of a mother standin' there." Sammy took another puff of his cigar and put his feet up on Charles's desk.

Charles grabbed Sammy's boots and lifted them up in the

air only to drop them on the floor. He jerked him up by wrapping his fists around the man's open lapels. "Keep your filthy feet off my desk. I'm particular about who makes themselves comfortable in my office. And you had better keep your hands to yourself around little girls in Crawford County, Sammy, and keep your mouth shut, too. If I have one more complaint, I'll personally throw you so far in jail you'll never get out. And I'll see to it that your jail duty is cleaning up the drunk tank every morning. You ought to feel right at home in the scum. Do you understand me?"

Sammy swallowed, his fat jowls quivering. "Yes," he squealed.

Charles dropped his hands, and Sammy sank back in his chair, sliding his fat body as far to one side as possible. "Now," said Charles in a conversational tone, "I understand you have a pilot's license."

Sammy licked his fat lips. "What's that got to do with the Jenkins girl?"

"Answer the question, Sammy," Charles said, putting his hands on the wooden arms of the chair and leaning over the shorter man.

"Yeah, I got a pilot's license," Sammy said, pulling his head back to escape the sheriff's close proximity.

"I understand you also knew Billy Joe Williams," Charles said, taking a blind stab in the dark.

"That piece of white trash!" Sammy scoffed.

"Don't insult your betters, Sammy."

"Now listen here, I don't have to take that kind of insult," Sammy said belligerently.

"You'll take anything I dish out and like it. You also knew Maria Martinez, didn't you?"

"Yeah, I know Maria Martinez. A hot little number if I ever saw one."

"How well did you know Maria?" Charles asked.

"What are you getting at, Sheriff? You can't get me about her; she's past the age of consent," Sammy sneered.

"She's also dead, Sammy. We took her body out of the barbecue pit yesterday. Do you mean you didn't know?"

Sammy's eyes veered away from Charles, and he licked his lips again. "Yeah, well I heard it somewhere, I guess."

"I'll ask you again, Sammy. How well did you know Maria?"

"She did some typing for me a couple of times. Then the snot-nosed L.D. Lassiter said I couldn't have her no more. Said my lewd talk upset her. Lewd talk, my hind leg. That little Mex was a tease. When I asked her to put out, she backed down. She didn't get nothin' she didn't ask for."

Charles grabbed a fistful of Sammy's shirt, bringing his face close down to his own. "Did you rape her, you lousy scum?" he shouted.

"Hell, no, I didn't rape her. I don't have to rape anybody. If she ever told anybody I did, she's a liar!" Sammy tried to pull Charles's hands away.

"That's not the story I hear, Sammy," said Charles, shaking the man.

"Damn it, she nearly ruined me, Sheriff. I couldn't do nothin' for a month. Kicked me right where I lived," Sammy cried, his eyes bugging out.

"It's too bad she didn't finish you off permanently, Sammy. So that's why you killed her? Did you want revenge because she humiliated you?"

"I didn't kill nobody, Sheriff!" Sammy shouted, fear making his voice wobble. "You can't prove I did!"

"You think not, Sammy?" Charles asked, dropping him back in the chair like a bag of grain. "What were you doing out on 1283 Saturday night?"

Sammy's face turned white as the color washed out. His eyes darted from side to side, seeking a way out. "That ain't any of your business, Sheriff," he spat out.

"I'm making it my business, Sammy. What were you doing out there? Did you meet Maria Martinez? Did she threaten you until you lost your temper and hit her? Or did you go out there planning to kill her?"

"I don't know what you're talking about, Sheriff. It wouldn't do her no good to threaten me. It was her word against mine about what happened. And who would believe a Mexican instead of me?"

"I would, Sammy, I would. There's some physical evidence in this case. And some very damaging evidence in Billy Joe's murder."

"What!" screamed Sammy. "What in hell has Billy Joe got to do with this?"

"Billy Joe saw you hit Maria, and he blackmailed you. I can tie you in to that one very easily," Charles lied.

"The hell you say! I didn't kill nobody. You just produce your evidence, Sheriff; it ain't worth a damn against me."

"I will, Sammy. Let's go down and look at your pickup."

"You ain't lookin' at nothin', Sheriff, without a warrant. And old Judge Pierce ain't gonna give you nothin' without a damn good reason. You're bluffin', and I'm a better poker player than you. I'm callin' your hand."

Charles folded his arms across his chest. "There's another hand being dealt, Sammy, and I'm going to have all the aces. You'd better come up with an alibi for Saturday, or I'm going to collect the pot and see you jailed for murder. I'm a dangerous man to cross, and you've stepped over the line once too often. Now get out of here. You're stinking up my office."

"You ain't heard the last of this, Sheriff. You can't push me around. I'll turn you in for mistreating a prisoner."

"You're not a prisoner, Sammy," Charles said. "Yet."

# CHAPTER

# 12

L.D. STUCK HIS HEAD AROUND THE CORNER OF THE door. "Should I throw my hat in first? Everybody in the department could hear you and Sammy. I thought you were going to kill him before you were through."

Charles wiped his hands on his slacks, trying to clean off the feel of Sammy's body. "God, I feel like I've touched something slimy."

"If you touched our illustrious J.P., you did," L.D. said, slipping into one of the wooden chairs and propping his feet up on Charles's desk. "I often wonder why no one has stomped on that fat cockroach."

"He admitted being out on 1283 Saturday night. He wouldn't give me any reason for being out there, just dared me to prove him guilty of murder. He also tried to rape Maria. She supposedly kicked him, but what if she did it after the fact. She could have called him when she found she was pregnant and threatened to expose him."

L.D. studied the toes of his boots for a moment. "Sounds good to me, Charles. He wouldn't think twice about killing someone if they threatened his little empire. As long as no one else knows about his proclivity for young girls, he's safe. He can wheel and deal, fix his friends' traffic tickets, take bribes, do whatever he wants to. But if he loses an election, then he loses his position of power. How did you find out where he was Saturday night? Did you have a witness after all?"

Charles looked uncomfortable. He didn't like lying even for a good reason. "I merely took a chance and asked him what he was doing on 1283 on Saturday, and he fell for it. I wish I did have a witness. My God, a person could kill half the county on one of these back roads at night and never be caught. I just don't have enough deputies to patrol nine hundred square miles of land.''

L.D. nodded in sympathy. "I know that, Charles. You'd need an army to keep a close watch on all the farms and ranches and roads in this country. Frankly, I wonder if you'll ever be able to arrest anyone for these murders.''

"I do have some evidence, L.D.; I have a cast of the tire tracks from the pickup used by Billy Joe's killer. But I just can't go checking anyone's tires without a warrant. If I do, then a defense lawyer can keep the evidence out of the trial because it was illegally obtained.''

Charles rose and paced his office in growing agitation. "There has to be a witness somewhere, L.D. People just don't bury themselves at night. If Sammy was driving down 1283 at night, then the chances are good someone else was, too.''

L.D. was quiet as he watched Charles's restless pacing. "I don't know, but I still think this one is unsolvable. Don't worry yourself into a case of ulcers. It isn't worth it.''

Charles stiffened and turned around to face his friend. "Isn't worth it! Is that what you said? For God's sake, L.D., two people were murdered, and you say it isn't worth worrying about! Two young people who still had their lives ahead of them! Just what in the hell do you think is worth worrying about?''

L.D. pulled his feet off the desk and straightened up. His eyes were chips of blue ice, frigid with anger. "Charles! That is enough! You're sounding obsessed with these murders. I'm not saying Maria and Billy Joe were worthless people. What I am saying is that you're not remaining objective. You aren't eating, you aren't sleeping. You're like a ground squirrel in a cage: running around and around, using up a lot of energy, and accomplishing nothing.''

L.D.'s voice grew persuasive, a lawyer trying to convince a jury. "Step outside your cage and view the whole thing from another angle. If you don't regain your perspective, you'll start twisting the facts to fit a pet theory. You must admit the possibility this case will never be solved. You are in danger of losing control, Charles. If that verbal exchange between you and Sammy is any indication, you've already lost it. You're on the verge of turning your investigation into a vendetta.''

''Maybe these murders deserve a vendetta, L.D.,'' Charles said, beginning to lose his temper. ''Maybe society is so interested in being in control that it is in danger of losing its humanity. Any society, any people, that doesn't lose control when faced with the crime of murder, is not a society I care to be a part of.''

L.D. raised eyebrows at the emotional outburst. ''Is that the real reason you left Dallas, Charles? Did no one get angry enough at the murder of your drug addict ex-wife? Is that why you decked your boss in the middle of the Adolphus Hotel lobby? Wouldn't he support your vendetta against the man you thought was guilty?''

Charles felt both vulnerable and angry at having his past exposed. ''You've obviously been snooping in my past, L.D., so I'll satisfy your curiosity: the D.A. didn't want a scandal in his department. So I compromised my principles and left. But I can promise you this: I'll never do it again.''

He braced his arms on his desk, letting his head hang loose. His stomach was burning like all the pits of hell. He could almost taste the acidity. He felt L.D. clasp his shoulder, and raised his head to meet the familiar eyes of his friend. The icy stare was gone as if it had never been there.

''Charles, I feel as angry as you do. But I'm also worried about you. I admit I expressed myself very badly, and I should never have mentioned what happened in Dallas, but in the last analysis, I guess I care more for you than I do about who killed Maria and Billy Joe. I don't want to see you become so obsessed that you flail everybody with your suspicions. I don't want a repeat of Dallas. I don't want you dropping out of this society because you think no one cares. Now sit down while I go get us a cup of that abominable liquid you keep referring to as coffee.'' He went out the door.

Digging his fingers through his hair until the coffee-colored strands looked windswept, Charles concentrated on his next step. He had been running this investigation without any organization. He had not stopped to assimilate the information he did have in his eagerness to gather more.

"Here you are," L.D. said, returning with two coffee cups and kicking the office door shut. "I don't know how you can stand this stuff. You must have a cast-iron stomach."

Setting Charles's cup on the desk, L.D. sank into a chair and propped his feet up. Taking a sip of the coffee, he grimaced with distaste. "This stuff is worse than ever."

Charles grinned. "It takes a real man to drink it, but you know how macho county sheriffs are."

"Macho, hell! You're just plain crazy. You could do tattoos with that garbage. Now tell me about the investigation." L.D. put his cup on the desk.

Charles shifted restlessly in his chair as he gathered his thoughts, arranged them in chronological order, and began talking. It was not a concise account, but was studded with his doubts and personal reactions. He digressed to describe Old Ben's arrest and Miss Poole's shower. His voice was heated as he described the interview with Sammy.

"He's subhuman, L.D.; he ought to be out swinging from the trees and picking lice out of his hair. I wish I could charge him with fondling the Jenkins girl, but I honestly believe his story. I like him as the murderer, but I can't blind myself to the possibility he's innocent. Perhaps I shouldn't say 'innocent'; I should say 'not guilty.' That degenerate wasn't innocent the day he was born."

L.D. sat looking at the map of Crawford County pinned to the wall behind Charles's desk. He shook his head as if to focus his thoughts. "As I see it, Charles, you're limiting your suspects to those that meet your criteria. It's a good theory, but without proof, it doesn't do you any good. Besides, those criteria could fit a lot of other people. You have no way of knowing how many people besides the service club knew the pit would be dug Saturday instead of Sunday."

"The murderer will make a mistake, L.D. And when he does, I'll be waiting."

"Not to change the subject too abruptly, Charles, but I have solved one of your problems," L.D. said, stretching his arms above his head and yawning widely.

"Oh, which one? The murder? Mabel the magnificent? Or how to teach Slim how to make decent coffee?"

"Nothing that complicated, I'm afraid. I talked to Old Ben, and I think you can let him out. God knows I've had experience with enough drunks as county attorney to recognize one who needs to be committed. There's nothing wrong with his thought processes; he's just conning you."

"I don't agree with you. There's something bothering him," Charles said, remembering the old man's actions.

"You'll have to let him out anyway; you don't have him charged with anything. He can't use the county jail as a flophouse. In fact, you ought to release him tonight. Technically, you can't keep him locked up any longer."

"I don't know, L.D., I was going to let him out tomorrow, but I think he's scared of something. But dammit, he won't talk."

"He didn't talk to me much either, but we can't play babysitter to an old wino. You're already over the limit, Charles. You've held him more than twenty-four hours without a charge. If some grubby Legal Aid lawyer gets hold of him, you can be sued for everything but your fillings."

"Old Ben isn't going to sue me, L.D. You're being ludicrous."

"Oh, hell, Charles," L.D. said in disgust. "Some lawyers are just like gunslingers; they're out to make a name for themselves. This would be a perfect case to build a reputation. Just think about poor Old Ben, helpless Old Ben, being imprisoned illegally by a bully of a county sheriff. Let him out, Charles."

Charles stared at his friend for a moment. L.D. was right: he was holding Old Ben illegally. But there had to be a way to both let him go and still keep an eye on him. He grinned suddenly. "All right, L.D.! I'll let him out, but there's no law that says I can't arrest him again in an hour."

"On what charge? Even Old Ben can't get drunk in an hour."

Charles shrugged his shoulders. "I'll think of something. Vagrancy would do, or loitering. He's an old man, and something's bothering him. The Sheriff's Department is the closest thing to a family he has, so I guess it's up to me to help him."

"Oh, for God's sake!" L.D. said, rising from his chair and striding to the door. "I wash my hands of the whole thing."

L.D. stopped, one hand on the doorknob. "Just promise me one thing."

"If I can," Charles replied, smiling at his friend a little sadly. It was the first time he and L.D. had disagreed so thoroughly, and Charles felt a sense of regret.

"Promise me you'll at least go down and get one of our famous hamburgers. You're going from lean to skinny, and I have to keep Carroll's most eligible bachelor in good shape. Just think of the votes I'd lose if the females of this town thought Angie and I weren't taking care of you. Now you don't want that to happen."

Charles laughed, feeling a buoyant release from the tension of the earlier conversation. "I promise," he swore solemnly. "I need to check on the bingo stand anyway. I may need to protect Miss Poole from Jim Bob Brown."

"Knowing Miss Poole, I think you need to worry about protecting Jim Bob. I'm working the hamburger stand tonight, so don't think you can avoid eating without my knowing."

"All right! All right! I'll eat. You're worse than a mother hen."

"That's because I'm scared of my wife. She gave me strict instructions to make sure you ate. You can blame her. Well, the hamburger stand calls. See you later."

Charles sat looking at the door, a silly grin on his face. He would eat a hundred hamburgers for Angie. He grabbed his hat off the filing cabinet on his way to the door.

Charles stopped at the dispatcher's desk and motioned to Juan. "Let Old Ben out. Tell him I can't keep him in jail any longer."

"Do you want me to take him home, Sheriff?" Juan asked.

"No. I'll arrest him later on tonight, so I don't want him wandering off by himself."

Juan and the dispatcher looked puzzled. "Why let him out if you want him in again?" Juan asked.

"It's a long story comprised of grubby lawyers, legal technicalities, and being a nursemaid." Charles waved his arm vaguely. "Never mind, Juan; just keep an eye on him. I'll be down at Frontier Days, either at the bingo booth or the hamburger stand."

Charles stood on the courthouse steps, surveying the celebration. The crowds were larger now, the squeals louder, the music more raucous. The benches around the bingo booth were full, leaving many people no choice but to sit on the grassy lawn with their bingo cards and a handful of dried corn as markers.

He leaned against one of the two-by-four boards holding up the roof of the booth. Jim Bob was on the microphone calling out the numbers, while Miss Poole collected each token and dropped it into another jar. Charles could hear the level of irritation in Jim Bob's voice rising with each token dropped into Miss Poole's jar. At the excited cry of "bingo," Miss Poole pedantically checked the numbers and handed over the prize selected by the winner. Prizes, from cheap ashtrays to radios and pocket calculators, were arranged in tiers in the center of the booth. Most winners could only choose a prize from the two lower levels. Several times a night a grand prize game was announced and the winner could select an article that might be worth fifty dollars or more.

Jim Bob clutched his head and groaned. He stepped in front of the sheriff and glared at him. "I think I'll kill you for getting me into this mess. I can't even get away from her in the men's john. I was sittin' in there havin' a smoke when this old geezer come in. Says Miss Poole is lookin' for me. I tell you, Sheriff, I'm going to be constipated until this thing is over."

"Jim Bob, I'm waiting," Miss Poole said. "We deserve a break, but we can't take all night. Sheriff, if you haven't eaten yet, you're welcome to join us."

Charles grinned. "Miss Poole, I'd be delighted." He could hear Jim Bob groan again. He slipped Miss Poole's hand through his arm and escorted her to the hamburger stand.

"Well, Sheriff, what will it be for you and your date?" Sammy asked with a leer.

Charles's eyes narrowed as he looked at the sweaty face of the J.P. "Two hamburgers and two Cokes. I see you took my advice and found a less dangerous place to work."

"We're not finished yet, Sheriff. I ain't sittin' in your office now," Sammy snarled.

"Better my office than the jail," Charles said. "Now get me

two hamburgers, and be sure they're wrapped before you touch them. I'm particular about who handles my food."

Sammy shot Charles a look of pure hate before turning his head to bellow the order to the cooks. Charles could see L.D. in a long white apron efficiently flipping meat patties on the grill. He pulled out his wallet to pay and looked up to see the tortured eyes of Leon McDaniels.

"That'll be three dollars and seventy-five cents, Sheriff."

Charles laid a five-dollar bill on the counter and waited for his change. He jerked his head up at the sound of a feminine voice.

"That's a dollar and twenty-five cents change," Geneva McDaniels said as she insinuated herself between her husband and the sheriff. Charles was reminded of a mother trying to protect her child as he met the hard eyes of Leon's wife.

Charles wordlessly took his charge and nodded at L.D., who came over with his order. "Here I am, L.D., just as ordered. You can tell Angie I ate my supper like a good boy."

"It's about time you followed orders, Charles. Did you let Old Ben out?"

"Yes, but I'm arresting him again this evening," Charles replied.

"That's your speed, Sheriff," Jim Bob said, masticating his hamburger like a cow chewing her cud. "You're too busy arresting drunks and worrying about old ladies to do something important like catch a murderer. Well, you better leave innocent people alone and find the guilty party."

"I'll catch him," Charles said, his glance passing from Jim Bob to Sammy to Leon. The trio met his eyes with varying expressions in their own. Jim Bob was angry, while Sammy responded with defiance. Only Leon's eyes seemed to hold regret. Charles found himself liking this quiet man and hoping he was not the killer.

"Oh, for goodness sakes!" Miss Poole exclaimed. "A blind man would know who murdered that poor girl. I certainly do."

# CHAPTER

# 13

THE FOUR MEN STOOD GAWKING AT MISS POOLE. "Close your mouths, gentlemen; the flies will get in. It never fails to amaze me that men can be so obtuse. You are acting as if you are totally shocked a woman could possibly figure out a murder. That's one of the reasons I never married. I never could find a man who gave me credit for having any intelligence."

Miss Poole wadded up her napkin and sipped her drink. "If you are ready, Jim Bob, I believe we'd better return to the bingo game."

"Not me, Miss Poole. I have to go to the courthouse a minute."

"I hope you will have your kidneys checked, Jim Bob; I suspect you may have a problem," Miss Poole replied as she hooked her hand through Charles's arm. "Will you escort me back, Sheriff? It's been such a long time since I've been in the company of a real gentleman."

Charles laid his hand over the frail fingers clutching his arm and walked slowly back toward the bingo booth. "Miss Poole, if you have any information about the murders, you must tell me. You made a very dangerous statement back there. Come up to my office, give me a signed statement, and I'll assign some deputies to guard you."

Miss Poole laughed, a merry, tinkling sound. "My goodness, Sheriff! You don't really believe I actually know the name of the murderer. That wasn't what I was referring to at all. I merely know the kind of person who must be guilty. He has to be a prominent citizen who would have a great deal to lose if anyone found out about his relationship with Miss Mar-

99

tinez. Obviously he also has to be a pilot, if gossip is correct and that poor Williams boy was killed by a spray plane. Unfortunately there are a lot of prominent men in this town who fly.'' Miss Poole took another sip of her drink.

"How do you know Maria had a relationship with anyone? How do you know that's why she was killed?''

"It's quite simple, Sheriff: there was no other reason to kill her. What chance did a Mexican girl have to find out any damaging information about anyone? Who would believe her if she did? No, this is a small town; we are still rather puritanical about sex. It's all right to indulge outside the marriage bed, but don't get caught, and don't make a fool of yourself. An affair with a young Mexican girl that resulted in pregnancy would be very damaging. I believe that this was the case, was it not?'' Miss Poole may have been a maiden lady but she was aware of the birds and the bees.

Charles stopped short and grasped Miss Poole's shoulders. "How did you know that?''

"Logic,'' Miss Poole said. "Logic tells me she must have been. A simple affair wouldn't have resulted in murder. I could be wrong on that point,'' she admitted. "But I believe an affair, while shameful, did not constitute a great danger. It would have been a case of her word against the man's. But a baby, particularly if it favors the father, is a little hard to argue away.''

Charles dropped his hands. "Your logic is impeccable, Miss Poole, but you can't go around in public claiming you know the identity of the murderer. It could get you killed.''

"You're dramatizing, of course, Sheriff. No one within hearing is intelligent enough to commit two murders.'' Miss Poole was quiet for a moment. "Except one, perhaps; I'll have to give that possibility some thought. I'll have to get back to work. Thank you for the hamburger.''

"Miss Poole,'' Charles insisted. "I'm going to assign a deputy to be with you until I can solve this case. You made a statement that could endanger your life, whether you meant it or not. I don't want another dead body in Crawford County.''

"If you insist, Sheriff. But don't you think I would be useful as a decoy, or red herring? You could stake out my house and catch the murderer when he tries to kill me. It would be a perfect trap.'' Miss Poole forced her hands under her chin, excitement lending a sparkle to her eyes.

Charles decided some young man forty years ago had missed getting himself one hell of a wife. ''Miss Poole, do you read mystery stories by any chance?''

Miss Poole ducked her head, a guilty flush giving color to her parchmentlike cheeks. ''I always wanted to be Miss Marple,'' she said shyly. ''Please, Sheriff. This will be my only chance to play detective.''

''There is nothing playful about a man who hides a live body in a barbecue pit, Miss Poole.''

She gasped, covering her mouth with one hand. ''Gracious, it's worse than I thought. You must use me now, Sheriff. It's the only way.''

''No, ma'am! You go run your bingo game, while I round up a deputy to guard you. And no more dramatic statements like you made before. This is not an Agatha Christie murder mystery.''

Charles gently shoved her into the booth. ''Now behave yourself, and don't leave without the deputy. Do I have your word on that? If you don't give me your word, I'll take you into protective custody and you can stay at the jail.''

Miss Poole pursed her lips, plainly disappointed. ''Oh, all right. You have my word. But remember; I'll be glad to help. I'm not a nervous nelly; I always keep my head in an emergency.''

''I'm sure you do,'' Charles said, smiling at the old woman. ''Now you stay right here until I send someone down.''

''Of course I'll be here. I gave my word,'' she said indignantly.

Charles climbed the courthouse steps and paused to look around. He saw Old Ben leaning against a tree, Juan beside him. No one seemed to be paying the old man any attention. He looked back at the hamburger stand but couldn't distinguish the faces. With everyone wearing identical white shirts, it was practically impossible to tell who was who from a distance. Giving up, he entered the courthouse and rode to the third floor, mentally trying to arrange a schedule that would allow one deputy per shift to ride herd on Miss Poole.

Stopping at the dispatcher's desk, Charles leaned over to check the duty roster. Damn, he thought, I can't spare Meenie or Raul from the day shift. With some hesitation he penciled a check by Slim's name. Maybe the coffee would improve temporarily if Slim was baby-sitting Miss Poole. Checking the evening shift, he decided on Juan Rodriquez. If an interpreter was needed, a city policeman could be called.

He tapped the pencil against his teeth. The midnight-to-eight shift was going to be difficult; the department was stretched thin during those hours. Most of the deputies spent their time patrolling the farm and ranch roads in an effort to prevent vandalism or theft of expensive farm equipment.

Charles could never remember with clarity hearing the shots. He knew he must have; even a twenty-two rifle makes some sound. He decided the noise of the carnival must have camouflaged the popping sound of the rifle. But the screams of the bingo players carried easily to the third floor. There was no question those screams conveyed shock and fear, unlike the cries of young girls pretending terror on the ferris wheel or a tilt-a-whirl. He dropped the pencil he was holding and ran to the staircase, his boots making rapid clicking noises on the tiled floor. He paused at the third-story landing and peered out the window, but the angle of view prevented his seeing the whole line of booths. He turned to the staircase, taking the stairs two at a time, feeling a terrible urgency. As he rounded the second-story landing, he caught sight of a man on the stairs below him.

"Stop!" he shouted, and saw the figure pause and turn a terror-stricken face toward him. The fluorescent lights above the stairs bathed the face in harsh starkness.

"Leon! Wait!" Charles almost fell in his haste to reach the man.

Leon stood on the steps, his broad shoulders slumping, hands covering his face. His arm was limp and unresisting and he followed docilely as Charles hurried down the last staircase to meet Juan's running figure.

"Sheriff, the lady is shot!" Juan was almost incapable of

being understood. His accent had thickened, becoming almost comical.

Charles thrust Leon's arm at Juan. "Take him upstairs and hold him. Call an ambulance and tell the dispatchers to get all the off-duty deputies back here." He didn't bother to ask who was shot; he knew. Miss Poole's impetuous statement had precipitated another murder. Charles hit the courthouse door, almost slamming the heavy obstacle against the side of the building in his haste. He ran across the lawn toward the bingo booth, unceremoniously shoving aside spectators, ignoring the bombardment of questions thrown at him by the crowd. He leaped over the short wall of planks into the booth itself, observing the men crouching on the floor like outlaws in a bad western.

He pushed aside two kneeling men and gently turned Miss Poole over, his hand going automatically to the side of her throat. He released a deep sigh as he felt a reedy pulse under his fingertips. Pulling a handkerchief out of his pocket, he pressed it against the obscene hole in the left side of her chest.

"Is she alive?" asked one of the men as he grabbed a decorative pillow off the prize table and wedged it under Miss Poole's head.

"Yes. The bullet missed the heart by a considerable distance, but I don't know if it caught the lung or not. Where in the hell did the shot come from?"

"I don't know, Sheriff. We were just calling out numbers and Miss Poole leaned over to check a winner's card, when she suddenly fell. I heard the popping sounds, and then I saw blood."

Charles felt as if a fist had connected with his stomach. There was only one other person who was afraid of something. He rose and frantically scanned the crowd, looking for Old Ben. His relief was almost tangible when he saw the old man leaning against the tree, his head lolling loosely on his shoulder. The incongruity of Old Ben's posture struck him forcibly a second later, and he vaulted over the wall of the booth and ran toward the old man. He was still several yards away when he saw the blood beginning to soak the old man's chest. The crowd had followed his progress, and a woman's piercing scream rent the night air.

Charles fell to his knees beside Old Ben, tears of regret and guilt trickling down his face.

He tenderly lifted Old Ben's hat from his head and stroked the old man's face. As his hand passed in front of Ben's lips, he felt a tiny bubble of frothy blood. Holding his breath, he felt a faint current of air. "My God," he said aloud. "The old man is alive!"

He felt a hand on his shoulder, then heard L.D.'s shocked voice. "Good God, how can he be alive? Look at all that blood."

Charles knelt down and unbuttoned Old Ben's shirt, peeling it off to bare the thin chest with its tiny blue-ringed hole. Blood seeped out with each shallow breath Old Ben took. "Missed the heart, but it looks like it hit the lung."

L.D. pulled a handkerchief out and held it against the wound in an attempt to stop the bleeding. "I'm sorry, Charles, I'm very sorry. If he dies, I killed him."

"Don't be ridiculous, L.D. You were right in everything you said; I was holding him illegally. It was my decision to let him out. I should have listened to my intuition. I knew he was scared of something."

The siren announced the approach of the ambulance. The crowd parted as the driver and an attendant, followed by a nurse, came running over with a stretcher. Charles rose and called, "Over here first."

The nurse dropped to her knees and quickly checked Old Ben. "I thought the victim was a woman," she said as she quickly applied a pressure pack to Ben's chest.

"The female victim is over at the bingo game. I don't think her wound is as critical as this one."

"My God, Sheriff," the driver said. "Did you have a shoot-out down here?"

"No, merely a murderer who is running scared. Can you tell me anything about the trajectory of the bullet?" Charles asked the nurse.

"Keep his head elevated," she said sharply. "From the froth around his mouth, it looks like we have a lung involved." She turned to Charles. "I don't know the answer to your question, Sheriff. You'll have to ask the doctor."

Charles felt Old Ben's back as the two men lifted him up. "I don't have to. The exit wound is lower than the entrance wound. The shot came from above."

He lifted his head and looked up at the courthouse. "The murderer had to have stood at a second-story window. The third floor on this side of the building is completely taken up by the jail." He glanced at the bingo game. Unconsciously, he lifted his head to the roof. From there, a quick shifting of his body would allow the murderer to make two quick shots at two different angles.

He heard more sirens as the off-duty deputies began arriving, and he saw Meenie threading his way through the crowd, followed by Raul.

"Meenie," he shouted, thinking he'd never been more glad to see his bowlegged, tobacco-chewing deputy. He drew Meenie to one side. "I think the shots came from the roof. Take a couple of deputies up there and see what you can find. Organize a search of the courthouse; I want that gun. I also want everybody detained who was in that building. Get hold of the police chief. Tell him I'm requesting the loan of one officer per shift to mount guard at the hospital. I need two men at all times, and I just don't have the manpower to do it. Put one deputy to grubbing around that tree and in the bingo booth for the bullets."

Charles turned to Raul. "Take as many men as you think you'll need and question this crowd. Pull in some police if you have to. I want to know if they saw anyone enter the courthouse prior to the shootings; more importantly, did they see anyone leave the courthouse after the shootings. I'm going to the hospital."

"I'll follow you in my car, Charles," L.D. said. "I want to unlock my office for the search."

Charles waved his hand absently and climbed into the ambulance. He hunkered down at the end of Old Ben's stretcher, trying to stay out of the way. The ambulance was crowded with two stretchers, the nurse, and the attendant. Both patients had oxygen masks on and pressure packs over the wounds. Charles braced himself as the ambulance turned a corner. "Are they both still alive?" he asked the nurse.

"The woman is doing fine, I think," she replied. "The old man is in very serious condition. What kind of nut would want to kill two old people, Sheriff?"

"I don't know, but if Old Ben pulls through this, I'm going to find out." Charles straightened and jumped out of the ambulance as its doors were opened. He stepped quickly out of the way as a nurse pushing a gurney appeared.

"You'll need another one," he said to a doctor already clad in a green scrub suit. "There are two victims."

"Good Lord," the doctor said. "Call up the surgeon, Nurse. We're going to need some help."

Charles leaned against the wall outside the operating room and wished he had never given up smoking. Two more people might die, and he still didn't have any evidence at all. He stared at the emergency room door. Miss Poole was still in there being prepared for surgery. Crawford County Hospital only had one operating room, and Old Ben was occupying it.

He leaned his head back against the wall, closing his eyes for a moment. The click of boot heels jerked him back from a somnolent state resembling sleep. L.D. came down the hall, a paper cup in each hand.

"Here," he said, thrusting a paper cup in Charles's hand. "Drink this; you look terrible."

Charles sipped thankfully, hoping the caffeine would clear the fuzziness that seemed to cloud his thinking. He saw the nurse's aide dragging three chairs down the hall, and pushed himself away from the wall to help her. Charles sipped the bitter coffee. "Did Meenie find the gun, L.D.?"

"No, he didn't. There were footprints on the roof—the killer wasn't very careful in that respect—but there was no gun. Meenie did catch Jim Bob in the toilet and Sammy up in his office. It appears as if all three of your suspects were in the courthouse at the right time. Meenie had them all rounded up. Mrs. McDaniels called their family lawyer, and he's been raising hell down there. Leon refused to talk to him, by the way. That man is at the breaking point; another push and he'll go over the edge. I hate to think of him as the murderer, but he's acting like a guilty man."

"I'll go back and start the questioning just as soon as I know Old Ben and Miss Poole will make it."

He hit his knee with his fist. "Damn that woman anyway, L.D. Her injury was totally unnecessary. She knew absolutely nothing except that the murderer must be a man with a great deal to lose. She also guessed Maria was pregnant. She said it was only logical to assume there was a good reason to kill Maria, that a simple affair was not enough motive. If she hadn't been so outspoken, she never would have been shot."

"What!" L.D. exclaimed. "My God! Her big mouth could have killed her."

"I know it, but she couldn't be persuaded she was in any real danger. She wanted to use herself as bait to catch a killer. She was bait, all right, and it just might have forced the murderer into his first mistake."

L.D. cocked his head to one side, a puzzled frown on his face. "How do you figure that? He seems to have acted quite intelligently so far."

"He tried to kill two more people. He's getting reckless; anyone could have seen him entering or leaving. He had to have taken that gun into the courthouse. Someone saw him. It's only a matter of time before I find that person."

"I don't think so, Charles. If a witness exists, he'd have said something immediately. No, the only mistake so far is Old Ben's still being alive." L.D.'s voice was convincing in its certainty.

"You're wrong there. The murderer's first mistake was getting Maria pregnant."

# CHAPTER

# 14

THE DOUBLE DOORS OF THE OPERATING ROOM opened, and Dr. Wallace appeared. Charles rose to his feet and stretched; the long hours of waiting had left him feeling stiff and old.

"The bullet punctured a lung, Sheriff," the doctor said, long grooves of fatigue on either side of his nose. "I don't know if he will make it or not; his age and general health are against him. I just can't tell you anything."

"When will he regain consciousness, Doctor? When will I be able to question him?"

"When I think he's strong enough to talk, I'll call you. Which will be in three or four days, or never. I just can't tell you."

"Someone tried to murder him, Doctor, and they'll try again. There'll be a guard posted at his door, and no one will be allowed in except the medical staff and myself. Call me as soon as he regains consciousness. I have to question him."

The doctor bristled. "I told you I'd be the judge of when he is able to answer questions. You'll talk to him when I say so, not before."

Charles's eyes locked with those of the doctor. "If you don't want to make a career of digging bullets out of bodies, Doctor, you'll call me when he wakes up. The murderer has struck four times in less than four days. By the way, there'll be a guard outside Miss Poole's room, also."

"You're turning this hospital into a prison ward, Sheriff." The doctor interrupted Charles's protest. "Oh, I understand the reasons, but I don't like it." The doctor turned away wearily. "I'll call you when he regains consciousness, Sheriff.

Now if you'll excuse me, I need to scrub for the next operation. God, what a night!"

Charles motioned to the city policeman. "Stay outside the door of Old Ben's room. Don't let anybody in; I don't care if the President wants to visit the old man, nobody gets in."

The police officer straightened like a soldier on parade. "Yes, sir. I understand."

"Fine. I'm going back to the courthouse. I'll send a deputy up to join you and arrange replacements from the midnight shift. L.D., drive me downtown."

"Sure, Charles," L.D. said.

The two men walked to the parking lot, their boots making crunching sounds in the gravel. Charles's legs felt wooden from fatigue and he sank down thankfully in the seat of L.D.'s pickup. "Where's your car?" he asked without any real curiosity.

"Angie's got the car. It's easier to haul the kids around."

Charles smiled, thinking of L.D.'s two children. Two little girls, ages three and three months, they were perfect replicas of their mother. "They're cute kids, L.D.," he said, rolling his head against the back of the seat.

"Yeah, they are, aren't they? I hope Angie will be able to handle the kids and still help with next year's campaign. I'm going to run for state representative, Charles. Can I count on your support?" L.D. glanced at Charles.

Charles thought about not seeing Angie for six months of the year and felt a wrenching of regret. "Yes," he said slowly. "I'll help you, but I hate to see you spend part of the year in Austin. I'll have to find somewhere else to eat Sunday dinner and watch the ball game."

"You need to get married, Charles. A bachelor politician is an object of suspicion."

"I'm not a politician, L.D., I'm a county sheriff who just happens to be an elected official. I haven't any ambition toward a political office; I'll leave that to you. When I lose an election, I'll hang out my shingle and be a lawyer again. I had all the ambitious wheeling and dealing I wanted in Dallas."

"Since I didn't grow up in Dallas, and didn't have the opportunities of a scion of a prominent family, I am ambi-

tious,'' L.D. said, turning a corner into the parking lot in front
of the courthouse. ''Crawford County isn't the whole world.
Besides, I like politics.''

''I don't,'' Charles said shortly. ''I like being able to look at
myself in the mirror without flinching.''

L.D. jerked his head around to stare at Charles, a small
muscle jerking in his jaw. ''Are you saying I can't?''

''I'm sorry, L.D. I didn't mean to lump you in with all the
politicians I've known. How does Angie feel about this?''
Charles asked, trying to picture her as a smooth, controlled
political hostess, and failing.

''She's not crazy about the idea,'' L.D. admitted. ''She'll
go along with me, but she'll have to learn a few lessons.
She's a little too frank and outspoken sometimes. That will
have to change.'' Charles felt depressed at the thought of
Angie changing.

As he climbed out of L.D.'s pickup and headed toward the
courthouse, he saw Raul and five deputies at the bingo game.
A small line of people were waiting in front of the booth. As
one person was released after being questioned by Raul or one
of the other deputies, another took his place. The carnival
booths were closed, as was the midway, but the hamburger
stand was still serving, mostly to the law enforcement people.
Charles veered toward the bingo stand.

''Raul, how's it going?''

Raul waved his hand at the remaining people. ''We're almost done, Sheriff, and I have found nothing. Several people
say they heard shots, and a couple of young men, Vietnam War
veterans, say the shots came from the courthouse. A couple of
men say they saw Sammy go to the courthouse just after Jim
Bob. But if someone used the door in the front or on the other
side of the building, no one at the celebration would have seen
them.''

''Finish up as quickly as you can and go home. I'll see you
tomorrow.''

''When will you go home, Sheriff?'' Raul studied Charles's
red-rimmed eyes.

''When the murderer is caught,'' Charles replied over his
shoulder as his swift strides carried him to the courthouse. He

and L.D. entered the building to find every office door un-locked and the lights blazing. Charles caught a deputy by the arm. "What the hell is going on?"

"Meenie is making us search the building again," replied the deputy. "He thinks the gun has to be here somewhere."

"But my office has already been searched once," L.D. said. "Did you at least put my records back in order? I've got a lot of confidential notes about my private practice in there, and I need to be able to find them when I need them."

"We haven't got to your office yet, Mr. Lassiter," said the deputy. "We started on the other end of the hall."

"I'm going to watch the search," L.D. said.

"Oh, for God's sake!" Charles said. "There's not a man on my roster I wouldn't trust. No one is going to read private notes and files, L.D. We're looking for a gun, not a purloined letter."

"I didn't mean to malign your staff, but I'm staying down here until they are through," he replied.

"Suit yourself, L.D.," Charles said, walking down the hall toward his cantankerous deputy. As usual, Meenie's Stetson was tightly clamped on his head, and the ever-present lump of tobacco swelled his cheek. Charles often wondered if Meenie dispensed with either item, even in bed. "What have you found?"

"Not a damn thing, Sheriff, except the bullet that hit Old Ben. Pried it out of the tree. Haven't found the one that hit Miss Poole. I don't know where the hell it went. The bullet we have is not good for much; it's pretty well smashed flat. I don't know if ballistics could use it or not. Of course, we got to find the gun first. I can't figure out where that gun is. The killer didn't have time to get out of the courthouse with it. You were out in the hall and the dispatcher and other deputy in the office headed toward the first floor to watch the doors just as soon as Juan got up there to tell them there had been a shooting." Meenie removed his hat to scratch the bald spot on the back of his head.

"Have you searched the grounds yet?"

"No, except for right around the courthouse where it woulda landed if someone had dropped it out a window. I wasn't too worried about anywhere else, 'cause a twenty-two, or any rifle for that matter, is a pretty big thing to carry around. It ain't like the killer could hide it in his pocket or under his hat and walk out the door with it.''

"When you finish here, go out and search every tree, shrub, bush, booth, whatever. That gun is around somewhere, and I want it found. I'm going to question our prime suspects. Give me your report when you finish. Oh, yes, go easy on L.D., will you? He's sure you're going to make a mess of his office.''

Meenie shifted his tobacco and spat into a sand-filled ashtray setting against the wall. "Hell, Sheriff, he was sitting right there when we searched it the first time, telling us to be careful with his papers. The boys didn't go nosing through anybody's private stuff. I don't know what he's so hot for. At least he's not cussing like Sammy.''

"Did you find anything in Sammy's office?''

"I didn't find no gun, Sheriff, but I did find about a thousand dollars in cash in his desk, and a list of people with an amount of money written alongside their names. Thought you might be interested in that.''

"I am interested, very interested,'' Charles said gleefully. "Where's the list and the money?''

"It's still in his desk, Sheriff. Hell, it wasn't a gun, so I couldn't just confiscate it. But I thought there was something funny about it.''

"Your instinct for something funny seems to be infallible, Meenie; I'll run up there and see if I can decipher what the crooked little bastard was up to. Somehow, I don't think those people on the list simply had borrowed money and were repaying it. Sammy wouldn't loan his own mother money, unless it was at twenty-five percent interest.''

"I hope we can get him on something, Sheriff. He's as crooked as a dog's hind leg,'' Meenie said in disgust.

Charles raised his hand in a salute and took the stairs two at a time, anxious to look at that list. Switching on the light in Sammy's office, he walked across to the desk. The middle drawer was open, as if there had not been enough time to close and lock it. He pulled the list out and scanned it. He whistled soundlessly to himself and reached for the telephone. Dialing a number, he began to smile. If his suspicions were correct, he was about to nail Sammy's hide to the wall.

"Hello, L.D.?"

The county attorney answered impatiently. "What are you calling me for? Your deputies are all over the office, doing everything but pulling up the carpet."

"Listen to this list of names and tell me if you have filed a petition to revoke their driver's licenses." Charles read the list of four names, than held his breath, waiting for L.D.'s reply.

"Yes, I did. All four have hearings in front of Sammy and the Department of Public Safety next week. I hope to hell Sammy doesn't grant probation again. Three of those guys picked up more tickets last month than I did the first ten years I had a license."

"I think you can count on probation for all four. Meenie found a list of those names and one thousand dollars in cash in Sammy's drawer. Each name had a amount beside it. It looks very much as if our friendly neighborhood J.P. was on the take."

"In my opinion, you have enough to take it to a grand jury, Charles, but check with our illustrious district attorney next time he decides to make an appearance in Crawford County. I've got to hang up; one of your deputies just pulled a file drawer out on the floor."

Charles heard the click of the receiver and hung up. He gathered the list and the money and walked upstairs to his own office. He slowed when he saw Mrs. McDaniels and her lawyer, Bill Davis, sitting on the worn leather couch in the foyer of the sheriff's department.

"Sheriff," said Mrs. McDaniels, "I demand you release Leon immediately. My lawyer, Mr. Davis, is prepared to file a writ of habeas corpus if necessary. He is also prepared to file suit against you and this county for false arrest."

"Mr. McDaniels is not under arrest; he's merely being detained for questioning. He may speak with his attorney at any time, but I believe he's indicated that he has no desire to do so. I certainly don't mind your waiting for Mr. McDaniels, nor do I object to his attorney's being present during questioning. However, it's his decision to make. Now if you'll excuse me,

I'll talk to your husband." Charles continued past the couch, but he paused when slender fingers wrapped themselves around his arm.

"Damn you, Sheriff, you will let him go, now. I demand it!" Geneva McDaniels's voice was shrill, her eyes wild and fearful.

Charles pried her fingers off his arm and motioned to the attorney. "Mr. Davis, if you could take care of Mrs. McDaniels, I'll speak with her husband. If he wants you present, I'll call you immediately."

Mr. Davis put his arm around Geneva McDaniels's shoulder and led her back to the couch. "Now, now, Geneva, you just let me take care of this." Patting her hand gently, he handed her a handkerchief and turned back to the sheriff. "I'm sorry about that, Charles," he said. "She's been under a strain lately. I know you'll call me if Leon desires. I don't understand why he doesn't want to see me, but tell him I'll keep everything I hear in strictest confidence."

"I'm sure he knows that, but I'll tell him anyway. Do you have any idea what the problem with Mrs. McDaniels is?"

"If I do, I wouldn't divulge it to you, not without permission," Davis said wryly.

"If you have knowledge of a crime, you can't legally refuse to tell me. Confidentiality doesn't extend that far," Charles said, knowing that lawyers seldom broke their vow of silence for any reason, legal or illegal.

"There's been no crime the law can prosecute, Charles; I will tell you that much."

"All right; I'll believe you." He called Juan over. "Bring Leon McDaniels to my office; then head over to the hospital and guard Old Ben's room. I'll send a replacement over from the midnight shift. And Juan, no one gets in to see him except me and the medical staff. If anyone tries, stop them."

Juan nodded his understanding. "I think if anyone tries too hard, I forget to speak English."

"Very effective, but not very original. Just growl at them and tell the hospital to call me."

"Okay, Sheriff," he said, grabbing his hat and heading for the jail to get Leon.

Charles straightened his shoulders and walked into his office, placing his hat in the usual place on the filing cabinet. Charles studied the man Juan escorted in. Leon McDaniels seemed shrunken, as if his tall frame had lost both inches and pounds. He sat leaning over with his forearms resting on his knees, his hands with their enlarged knuckles clasped loosely together.

"Leon," asked Charles quietly, "why were you in the courthouse just after the shooting?"

Leon cleared his throat as if there were some obstruction preventing his speech. "I heard what Miss Poole said, Sheriff. I was coming to ask you who she accused. I have to know, don't you see? I can't live knowing there was someone else she loved. I have to know who hurt her."

"What would you do if you knew his name, Leon?"

"I would kill him," Leon said simply. "No one should have hurt Maria." He stopped a moment, struggling with tears. Charles turned his chair to watch the door, not wanting to embarrass the man by witnessing his anguish. "I would have helped her, Sheriff; I would have married her and raised her child as my own. Why didn't she come to me? Why didn't she?" he cried, clutching the edge of the desk, searching Charles's face for answers.

"Perhaps she didn't love you, Leon. Perhaps she did love the baby's father and thought he would help her. Or perhaps you are the baby's father . Did she come to you, Leon, and ask for help? Did you kill her so no one would know you had been sleeping with a Mexican girl young enough to be your daughter?"

"It couldn't have been my baby, Sheriff. I'm sterile."

Charles jerked upright in his chair. "Can you prove that, Leon?"

"Yes. My doctor, or any doctor you choose, will verify it. I've known for years. So you see, I wouldn't have killed Maria because I feared her pregnancy."

Charles groped for sound footing. Leon no longer fit into his criteria unless his motive were jealousy. "Did you kill her because she was pregnant by someone else? Did she come to you for help, and you killed her because you were jealous?"

"No, Sheriff, I told you, I would have married her. I've always wanted children. I even wanted to adopt, but Geneva wouldn't agree. I would have gladly raised Maria's child. I knew how ridiculous it was for a forty-five-year-old man to be in love with a seventeen-year-old girl, but I didn't care. In fact, if I'd known about her pregnancy, I'd have been happy. It would have meant she would stay here with me. I was going to pay for her education, even knowing she would never come back home. But that didn't matter, because I wanted her to be happy. I wouldn't ever have done anything to hurt her, Sheriff. You must believe that," he said earnestly.

Charles sighed. He hoped this kind man hadn't killed Maria. "I'll have to check your truck tires, Leon, to see if they match the cast we took. I take it you will agree to that?"

"Yes, Sheriff. Look at all my tires if you want. But please tell me one thing: who did Miss Poole accuse?"

"No one, Leon. She was speaking generally of the type of man who would have killed Maria."

"Oh, my God!" Leon exclaimed. "Someone shot that poor woman because of a mistake. That's horrible! If you knew me better, you would realize even if I'd killed Maria, I wouldn't be able to kill anyone else just to protect myself."

Charles rose and held out his hand. "Leon, I hope I can look forward to knowing you better." The two men shook hands. "Your wife is waiting outside; she's been very anxious."

"Yes, I'm sure she has. I'm also sure that this tragedy has pushed me into a decision I should've made years ago. Perhaps if I had, Maria would be alive and married to me. Divorce is like a death, Sheriff, but sometimes it is the only course to be taken. Thank you for your kindness. And thank you also for not being disgusted with my feelings for Maria."

Charles thought of Angie. "I can understand wanting something you can't have. And I never ridicule it under any circumstances." He watched as Geneva McDaniels threw herself into her husband's arms, desperation twisting her face until it looked drawn and ugly.

Charles motioned to a night shift deputy, an older man with several years' service in the department. "Rusty, take over from Juan at the hospital. Slim will relieve you in the morning.''

"Okay, Sheriff," Rusty Maclean said. "I'll hold down the fort until Slim gets there." Charles turned to Sammy, waiting for him besides the dispatcher's desk. "All right, you crooked bastard, you can cool your heels a while longer. I'm going to visit with Jim Bob a few minutes first.''

Sammy turned to Jim Bob and said viciously. "You keep your mouth shut, you fool, or I'll take you down with me.''

"Shut up, Sammy," Charles roared. "Jim Bob, go in my office; I'll be there in a minute." He watched the tall man uncoil himself from his chair and walk into the office, then turned back to Sammy. "I may be satisfied with what I've found out tonight, Sammy boy, but if you push me I'll look a little deeper. I think a stretch in prison at Huntsville would do you an immense amount of good.''

Sammy glared at Charles, his eyes guarded. "Go to hell, Sheriff.

"I don't think so, Sammy. I don't care to share accommodations with you." Charles grinned at the spiteful look on Sammy's face.

# CHAPTER
# 15

CLOSING HIS OFFICE DOOR, CHARLES WALKED OVER to his desk. He sank into his chair and folded his hands. "Jim Bob, what were you doing in the courthouse?"

Jim Bob flushed. "Hell, Sheriff, I had to go to the can; you know that. My God, you're worse than Miss Poole. A man can't even take a crap in private anymore."

Charles arched an eyebrow in disbelief. "Are you telling me you were in the bathroom from the time you left Miss Poole and me until the deputy detained you after the shooting?"

Jim Bob's eyes slid away from Charles. He wet his lips and grinned. "I told you I was constipated."

Charles uttered a short laugh. "Come on, Jim Bob. Either you take the longest potty breaks in history, or you're lying. And I suspect you're lying. I think you made a little trip up to the roof and took a shot at Miss Poole and Old Ben. You need to practice; you didn't kill either one."

"Hell, Sheriff, I can't stand old lady Poole, but I ain't gonna shoot her. I might strangle her, but I ain't gonna shoot her. And why in hell would I kill Old Ben? Why would anybody want to kill those two?" Jim Bob sounded genuinely puzzled.

"Didn't you hear Miss Poole make her declaration about knowing who murdered Maria?" Charles asked.

"Yeah, I heard her; the whole hamburger stand heard her." Jim Bob stopped, as if enlightenment had suddenly struck him. "Oh, I see; the murderer heard her and decided to close the old woman's mouth. I've got news for him: it'll take more than a bullet to shut up Miss Poole. She's a tough old bird. But I didn't kill nobody, so I don't care if she takes out an ad in the

118

paper announcing who the murderer is. It ain't got nothing to do with me."

"Very convincing story, Jim Bob. You've only got one problem I can see."

"What's that, Sheriff?" asked Jim Bob.

Charles stared at him, his brown eyes condemning. "I don't believe a damn word of it. Now, let's start over. Why were you in the courthouse?"

"I told you why," Jim Bob replied doggedly. "I was in the can."

Charles raised his hand, fingers outspread; as he ticked off each point, a finger curled down. "You have no alibi for Saturday night; you knew Maria; you can fly a spray plane; you knew about the barbecue pit being dug on Saturday; and now you appear in the courthouse, again without an alibi, during the time of two attempted murders. You'd better come up with a better story, or I'm going to arrest you on suspicion of murder."

Jim Bob stared at the sheriff's hand, now clenched in a fist. "You can't arrest me! You got no proof!" he shouted, half rising from his chair.

"Sit down, damn it!" Charles ordered. "I do have some physical evidence, and now I have enough probable cause to get a search warrant. You're in for a lot of embarrassment, Jim Bob, even if it turns out you're innocent."

The silence in the room stretched into minutes, and still Jim Bob didn't move. He looked at Charles and licked his lips, seemed about to speak, than suddenly shook his head stubbornly.

Charles leaned forward. "Shall I help you, Jim Bob? You stopped by Sammy's office after you left the hamburger stand. How long before our sleazy J.P. appeared?"

Jim Bob's head jerked up, his eyes wide with shock. "About five minutes," he replied in a resigned voice.

Charles smiled grimly to himself. "What happened after you paid him the three hundred dollars?"

"I went back to the bathroom." Jim Bob sat staring at the floor.

"Is that where you hid the gun?"

Jim Bob's fist slammed against the heavy oak desk. "I didn't shoot them! I didn't have any gun!"

"How well did you know Maria?" asked Charles relentlessly, ignoring Jim Bob's gesture of defiance.

"She did some typing for me. I liked her, but I don't mess around with young girls. You ought to be asking Sammy; he likes them young."

"Oh, I'll get to Sammy, don't worry about that. Why were you out on 1283 Saturday night?" Charles thought if the ploy worked once, it might work again.

Jim Bob stiffened, then nervously looked around as if he feared being overheard. "How the hell do you know that?" he asked in a panicky voice.

Charles felt elated; it *had* worked again. "Let's just say I have it on good authority—an impeccable source, so to speak. Now, suppose you answer the question."

"I ain't saying another word without a lawyer," Jim Bob said, folding his arms across his chest.

If Jim Bob wanted a lawyer, then he was running scared. Charles leaned back in his chair, his body seemingly lax. "If you're innocent of murder, you'd better tell me why you were driving along 1283. As it stands now, I can charge you with murder. If you weren't busy killing Maria, then you'd better tell me what you were doing."

"Damn it, Sheriff! I didn't kill Maria! You've got to believe me!" Jim Bob was beginning to sound desperate.

Without warning, Charles changed the direction of questioning. "Why were you late getting to the barbecue pit Sunday morning, Jim Bob? Did you have to kill Billy Joe first?"

Jim Bob stepped neatly into the trap. "A lot of people were late, Sheriff; six o'clock is awful early. Sammy was late, even Leon McDaniels was late. Hell, I don't think anybody was there right at six. That doesn't prove a thing."

"Not by itself it doesn't," Charles agreed. "Taken together with everything else, it looks damning. I've already got you on a bribery charge; I can hold you on that while I do a little more investigating."

"You're gonna ruin me, Sheriff!" Jim Bob cried.

"You're doing a good job of that yourself, you don't need

my help. Are you going to tell the truth, or am I going to lock you up?''

"Sheriff, I didn't kill Maria, and you can't prove I did. You've got no witnesses.''

Charles shook his head slowly. "I don't need witnesses. I can make a damn good case from circumstantial evidence. Plus I have the cast of the tire track we found at the airport, the one from the murderer's pickup.''

Jim Bob's face lightened, and he leaned back in his chair, seeming nonchalant. "Sheriff, you just run right out and check the tires on every vehicle I own. You can forget about a murder charge, 'cause you ain't got a case. As for bribery, I don't think you'll get far on that either. Everybody in the county knows you can buy your way out of losing your license in Sammy's court. I don't think a jury would do much more than slap my wrist.''

Charles sat staring at Jim Bob. "Have you put new tires on your pickup?''

"Nope,'' Jim Bob said, pulling out his pocket knife and cleaning his fingernails. "You know, Sheriff, I'm tired of you harping at me about killing Maria. To tell the truth, I'm tired of your being on my back. It's harrassment, that's what it is.''

Charles's eyes narrowed. "What bothers you, Jim Bob? My questioning you about Maria? You were a little upset yesterday, a little indignant, but you weren't calling for a lawyer, and you weren't screaming harrassment. As a matter of fact, you didn't call for a lawyer until I asked you why you were on 1283 Saturday night. Are you scared because you killed Maria, or because you think I'll find you were doing something else?''

Jim Bob shifted uneasily in the hard wooden chair. "Just check my damn tires and get off my back, Sheriff. I didn't kill Maria, and that's all you need to know. You ain't got no right to go digging into my business.''

"I think I'll make your business my business, Jim Bob. You aren't off the hook yet. I'll send Meenie home with you to check out you tires. And I still want to know what you were doing Saturday night. I'm a very curious man.''

Charles rose and walked to the door. "After you, Mr. County Commissioner,'' he said sarcastically.

Jim Bob pulled his bandanna out of his pocket and wiped his face, unaware that the sheriff heard his sigh of relief. "Get your deputy. I got nothin' to hide."

Charles looked around the outer office, spotting Meenie with one skinny hip perched on the dispatcher's desk. He jerked his head at his deputy, then turned back to Jim Bob, his face cold. "You're hiding something, all right, and you're being a fool about it. I'm assuming whatever you were doing is illegal or immoral or both. Unless you were hurting someone else, I would probably have ignored it. But I won't now. I don't like being lied to; it makes me mad."

"What do you want, Sheriff?" Meenie, shifting his tobacco and aiming at a spitoon beside the dispatcher's desk. The deputy looked tired, his straggly, grizzled beard limp.

"Have you finished the search?"

Meenie looked at Jim Bob and moved away. Charles followed him. "Yeah, and there ain't a gun in or around this courthouse. We even looked in the light fixtures, and practically took all the desks apart. Slim pulled out a drawer in L.D.'s office, spilled papers everywhere. I never knew L.D. was a cussin' man."

"Did L.D. go home?" Charles asked.

Meenie looked disgusted. "Hell, no! He's down there straightening out his office, still cussin'. He's almost as good as Sammy, only cleaner."

Charles shrugged his shoulders. "He'll get over it. L.D. never stays mad for long. Listen, grab that cast we made and go home with Jim Bob. He's decided to let us compare it with his pickup."

"That's big of him. What did you have to do, twist his arm?"

"In a manner of speaking," Charles said. "Tomorrow morning go out to Leon's and check his vehicles."

Meenie rubbed his sparse beard. "Sure hope I don't find nothin' at his place. Never did like the idea of it being him."

"I don't like it either, Meenie," Charles agreed. "But I'm sure we can scratch him off the list."

"Okay, Sheriff. I'll see you tomorrow. Are you going to Maria's funeral?"

Charles sighed. "I guess I'll have to go. I don't necessarily believe that old saying about the murderer showing up at his victim's funeral, but I'm clutching at straws. If something doesn't break soon, I'm going to confess myself, just to solve the case."

"Maybe Miss Poole or Old Ben will be able to tell you something," Meenie said, shifting his wad of tobacco to his other cheek.

Charles shook his head unconsciously. "Miss Poole doesn't know anything; she just said the wrong thing in the wrong place. And Old Ben may not make it."

"He sure as hell must know something, or the killer wouldn't have bothered to shoot him," Meenie said.

"I hope he lives long enough to tell me," Charles said, hitting the palm of his hand with his fist.

Meenie lifted his hat and scratched his bald spot. "I don't know how he coulda seen the murder. 1283 is a long ways from his box car shanty. But he might have seen the murderer dump the body; the barbecue pit ain't but a half mile or so from his place."

"No, it's not. It must be two miles or more from his shanty to the pasture," Charles objected.

Meenie shrugged. "If you go by the road, yeah. But if you're walking, like he generally does, it's a lot closer."

"I didn't know that. I'm still thinking in city terms of blocks and streets. My damn ignorance of this county nearly killed two people. I don't have any business as sheriff, Meenie. I don't know enough about the lay of the land."

"No one else could do as good as you, Sheriff. You're a fair man, and you know the law. You'll learn what you need to know about this county." Meenie reached up and squeezed Charles's shoulder, an unexpected gesture from that undemonstrative man.

"How many more people are going to die while I'm serving my apprenticeship, Meenie?" Charles asked bitterly.

"They would've died anyway, Sheriff. Stop standing around blaming yourself and do some thinkin'; that's what you do best anyhow. It's thinkin' that's going to solve this case, not whether you know who owns a particular cornfield."

Jim Bob's voice broke into their soft-spoken conversation. "Sheriff, are you sending me home or not? I got to work tomorrow."

"Meenie, follow him home. Jim Bob, remember what I said. I won't stop until I know everything, including what kind of underwear you like."

Charles turned away and stood gazing at Sammy. If you scratched off Jim Bob, he was his last, best suspect. He wanted Sammy to be guilty; he was such a greasy, disreputable piece of dung. "Come on, let's get this over with."

Carefully closing his office door, Charles crossed the room to stand directly in front of Sammy. "Well, look whom my deputies found skulking in the stairwell after the shooting. Would you care to explain what you were doing?"

"I don't have to explain anything to you, Sheriff. I'm an elected official of this county. I've got a right to be in the courthouse."

Charles put his foot on the edge of Sammy's chair and leaned over, resting his forearms on his knee. "Do you often conduct official business at seven-thirty in the evening, Sammy?"

Sammy shifted his body, trying to move as far away from the sheriff as possible without actually changing chairs. "I had some things to catch up on, some paperwork."

"Your paperwork didn't happen to have four names on it, did it?" Charles asked, his voice very soft and seemingly unconcerned.

Sammy wiped his hand across his balding head as if searching for hair. "I don't know what you're talking about."

"Did the paperwork happen to deal with money in any way?" Charles asked, his voice still soft.

"What's all this talk about money and names?"

"Would your paperwork have anything to do with probation instead of the loss of a driver's license?" Charles waited with seemingly infinite patience.

"You can go to hell, Sheriff, you and Jim Bob both. I'm not answering any more questions. You're trying to ruin my reputation with some kind of false bribery charge. Well, you aren't going to get by with it." Beads of sweat were sprinkled on Sammy's bald head.

"Now did I mention Jim Bob and a bribery charge?" Charles asked innocently. "I don't remember doing that, but it's entirely possible that I did. I sometimes forget things if I don't make myself notes. Do you ever make yourself notes, Sammy? You know, just a little reminder on a memo pad, perhaps?" Charles quirked one eyebrow, and smiled.

"You can't prove a thing, Sheriff," Sammy said, licking his fleshy upper lip.

"Oh yes I can. I have enough to take to the grand jury. I'm about to close down your little racket. I'm going to lock you up tonight. It's too bad the judge is out of town; you may have to stay in jail a couple of days until your bond can be set," Charles said, removing his foot from Sammy's chair and circling around his desk to sit down.

"That damn Jim Bob Brown; I'm going to see him fry for this. He offered me a bribe. That makes him as guilty as me. Why aren't you arresting him? How come he got to walk out of here?" Sammy's face twisted, a hunted animal turning to attack.

Charles lied without a qualm. "Jim Bob was very cooperative. Now suppose you tell me what you were doing during the time of the shootings?"

Sammy's lip curled up in a snarl. "I ain't telling you anything!"

Charles levered himself out of his chair. "You leave me no choice then. I'm giving you Old Ben's cell. Since you shot him, he won't need it for a while."

"I didn't shoot that old drunk, or the old biddy either. I stayed in my office until I heard you thundering down the stairs," Sammy shouted.

Charles looked skeptical. "Is that so? I didn't see you."

"You were too busy chasing Leon. Then your deputy came running up with Leon in tow. I left my office and started downstairs to see what in hell was going on. I heard the back staircase door open and someone run down the hall. By the time I got to the first floor, he had disappeared. Then your damn deputies caught me and hauled me upstairs. I don't appreciate being treated like a crook, Sheriff.'' Sammy straightened up in his chair, a pious look on his face.

"Get used to it, Sammy. Everyone in prison is treated like a crook. Now, how do you know this mythical person you say you heard was a man?''

"There ain't nothing mythical about him. Damnation! A man gets accused of lying even when he's telling the truth.''

Charles smiled sarcastically. "I wondered why you had such a pained expression on your face. It must hurt to tell the truth after a lifetime of lying. Now how do you know it was a man?''

"He wore boots. It's real hard to run quietly when you wear boots.''

"Most of the men in this county wear boots, and half the women. You can do better than that,'' Charles retorted.

"A woman damn sure didn't get Maria Martinez pregnant. I may not be a smart college graduate like you, but I can add two and two. Whoever shot Old Ben and that witch also killed Maria. Wasn't a woman who killed Maria,'' Sammy said, a self-satisfied look on his face.

Charles felt a moment of unwanted admiration for Sammy's logic. "You sound certain, as if you knew who the murderer is. Was it you, Sammy? Did you kill her because she got pregnant when you raped her in your office? Is that how you know it was a man out in the hall? Because you were that man?''

"Hell, I didn't rape her. I don't need to rape no woman,'' Sammy snarled.

"Not as long as you can pay pimps for young girls. That's right, isn't it, Sammy?'' Charles asked, slamming the palm of his hand on his desk.

"Yes! Yes! Yes!'' Sammy screamed. "No one can hold that against me. Everyone goes to a prostitute sometimes.''

Charles sank back in his chair and curled his lip. "Not the men I care to associate with.''

"Not everybody can look like you, Sheriff. Not everybody is born with a silver spoon in his mouth,'' Sammy said sullenly.

"That really has very little to do with it. A little kindness works better than looks or money. You ought to try it some-time. Say in about five years, when you get out of jail.''

"I'm not going to jail. No jury is sending me to jail for fixing a few traffic tickets.''

Charles smiled wolfishly. ''They will for murder, Sammy, and you're still a good suspect. You don't have an alibi for Saturday night, and you won't give a reason for being out on 1283.''

"I got an alibi, I'm just not going to use it unless I have to. There are other people involved,'' Sammy said pompously.

Charles snorted. "You never considered another person in your life, and this isn't the time to start. I suggest you tell me where you were and what you were doing.''

"I'm not telling you anything, not anything. You aren't going to arrest me for murder; you've got no proof.'' Sammy folded his arms and slouched back in his chair, staring defiantly at Charles.

Charles braced his hands on his desk. "That's where you're wrong, Sammy. I'm going to arrest you, but not for murder—at least, not yet. I may add that charge, too, but not at the moment. I'm placing you under arrest for suspicion of taking a bribe.''

Charles walked to the door and, opening it, surveyed the other room, now crowded with a milling group of deputies and city police. "Raul, come here,'' he said as he spied the slim figure of his deputy.

Raul detached himself from a group of city police and walked over, fatigue plainly evident in the dark smudges under his eyes. "Yes, Sheriff,'' he said, pushing his hat to the back of his head.

"Raul, you have the privilege of booking Sammy for suspicion of taking a bribe. Let him call his lawyer, then lock him up. Treat him gently, please. He's the type to scream police brutality if he stubs his toe on the cell door.''

Sammy stood in the doorway, his mouth gaping open. Raul motioned him toward a desk in the far corner of the squad room. For a moment it seemed he would follow docilely, but that illusion was shattered as he lunged for the waiting room.

"No, by damn! You're not locking me up! Not me!" he screamed.

A burly deputy from the night shift grabbed him from the back, pinning Sammy's flailing arms against his body. "The desk is over this way," he said, muscles bulging in his arms as he picked up the shorter man and carried him over to the desk. Charles hoped he wouldn't have a hernia as a result of picking up Sammy's fat body.

"My God, Charles," L.D. said, as he shouldered his way through the deputies to the sheriff's side. "You really did it. I'm surprised Sammy's not in a state of shock. A sheriff actually dared to step in and wreck his little empire. Congratulations."

"Why hasn't someone done it before? Why didn't you, L.D.? Evidently everyone knows about his crooked dealings."

L.D. shrugged his shoulders. "Oh, I'd heard about him. It's one of those things you learn at your mother's knee, along with the alphabet. The problem was getting any proof. You are the first one to manage that. If nothing else ever comes of the murder case, you at least eliminated one leech on society."

"I did more than that. Now I can get a warrant to search for more evidence of bribes. In the process I can check the tires on his pickup and see if they match the cast. I may find he's guilty of murder, too."

"Are you sure you're not using the bribery charge just to prove him guilty of murder?" L.D. asked with a grin.

Charles shook his head. "By a process of elimination, L.D., he almost has to be guilty. If he isn't, I may find myself in the position of having no suspects."

L.D. frowned at Charles. "What about Jim Bob and Leon? How did you manage to eliminate them?"

"Leon was in love with Maria; also, both he and Jim Bob gave me permission to check their tires. And most important of all, Leon couldn't have impregnated Maria: he's sterile."

L.D. shook his head sorrowfully. "That gives him an even better motive. He was jealous. His sweet little Maria was sleeping with someone else and got pregnant. She tells Leon about it, asks him what to do, and he kills her in a fit of jealous age. I like Leon; I think he's a good man. But even a good man can lose his temper if he's pushed far enough.''

"I don't think he would let me check his vehicles if he were guilty. Besides, you didn't hear him talk about Maria, I did. He was genuinely in love with her.''

"You give love too much credit. I never thought of you as a romantic before, but you are. Love can be destructive as well as constructive. Imagine what a blow it must have been to Leon's ego to realize Maria was sleeping with someone else.''

L.D. shook his head again. "I don't care what your check of his vehicles shows, Charles. Tires are a dime a dozen around a big farm. Everyone has a spare in the barn, or the implement shed, or on the back of his pickup. Not only that, but Angie heard about that cast at the beauty shop this morning.''

"What!'' interrupted Charles. "How in the devil did anyone find out?''

"You forget how small the town is. Everyone knows everyone else, or at least knows someone who knows someone else. I believe it was the kid at the airport that spilled the beans.''

"Damn it! Isn't anything a secret in this town?''

"Very little, Charles, very little,'' L.D. said sympathetically.

# CHAPTER

# 16

CHARLES STOOD IN FRONT OF THE CATHOLIC church thinking how much he hated going to funerals. They seemed such a cold, ritualistic way to bid farewell to the dead. He had always felt a good Irish wake was a much more positive way to do it. He wondered if he could leave instructions in his will for a three-day wake filled with feasting and toasting, followed by a funeral procession down Main Street with the Carroll High School band playing "Ghost Riders in the Sky." That would be the only fitting way for a county sheriff to go.

Charles took off his Stetson as he stepped into the church. The mourners were mostly Mexican, with only a sprinkling of Anglos. Many of Maria's teachers, several people from the courthouse, including L.D. and Angie, and the McDaniels, were seated near the front. He saw Raul and Meenie sitting on a back pew and slid in next to them. "Is Jim Bob here?" he asked in a whisper.

"Yeah," Meenie said, making an unconscious shifting motion of his jaw. Charles stared at him, puzzled by something unfamiliar about his face. Meenie flushed a dusty red. "I spit out my chew before we came in. I don't rightly know how to act."

Charles bit the inside of his cheek to prevent a smile. Seeing Meenie without a cheek rounded out by a wad of tobacco was almost like seeing a preacher in a cat house: it probably happened, but no one ever witnessed it. "Where is Jim Bob?" he asked, then looked straight ahead to avoid seeing Meenie's helpless manipulating of a nonexistent wad.

130

"He's sitting on the other side. I think the editor of the paper is right next to him. I didn't know they were friends."

"Jack is doing a little checking for me," Charles replied vaguely. "I see Leon brought his wife."

Meenie shifted his mouth before catching himself. "Yeah, and I think she must be mad as hell, too. She stomped in here and flung herself down. Didn't speak to the Martinezes at all. Leon was embarrassed. She's kind of strange, Sheriff; always was."

Charles studied Geneva McDaniels, observing the rigid set of her shoulders and neck. He wished he could see her face. "Where was she on Saturday night, Meenie?"

The deputy looked startled for a moment, then stared at Leon's wife, an expression of self-disgust on his face. He moved his shoulders as if shrugging off the last of his illusions about the human race. "Hell, I don't know. Leon just said she was visiting friends and couldn't alibi him. I never checked on her."

"She knew her husband was in love with Maria; she might have been afraid Leon was planning to divorce her to marry the girl. Maria was small, and Mrs. McDaniels is much taller, and probably stronger. We don't know Billy Joe was calling a man that night, we only assumed he was. Does she have a pilot's license?"

Meenie nodded his head. "I think so, and I know damn well she can shoot. As a matter of fact, she's won a lot of trophies. Did she overhear Miss Poole spouting off last night?"

"Yes, and I never thought anything about it at the time."

"There's only one catch: Leon's vehicles all checked out. None of the tires matched."

"According to L.D., that doesn't prove a thing. It seems that our making a cast has already made the rounds of the beauty shops. The kid at the airport told his mother, who presumably told her friends. I was hoping our suspects hadn't heard it, but it seems I was wrong."

Meenie scratched his scraggly beard. "That figures. I've lived around here for a long time, and I ain't never known anything to stay a secret long."

Charles rubbed his face. It felt stiff with fatigue. "I don't know where to go from here, Meenie. This case sounded so easy when I started, but everything is falling apart. My own stupidity about Old Ben is unforgivable. I'm beginning to think L.D. is right about it being impossible to catch the murderer.''

"We're always a damn sight smarter when we use hindsight, Sheriff. But we got to do the best we can at the time. You stand around worrying about what can be helped. Just forget it and go on.''

Charles smiled at his deputy. "Quite a philosopher, aren't you, Meenie?''

"If you say so, Sheriff.''

Charles settled back as the priest appeared and the mass began. He focused his eyes on the metal casket and wondered how the family could afford such an elaborate one. He watched Leon sitting stiff and still in his pew and realized that McDaniels must have contributed, probably without the knowledge of the family. Mr. Martinez would have considered such charity an affront to his pride.

Charles followed the unfamiliar funeral ritual, imitating Raul's actions. He shifted uncomfortably on the pew and unconsciously sighed when it was over. He stood and filed out with Meenie and Raul, waiting on the sidewalk for the church to empty. He couldn't say what he was waiting for—perhaps to catch a glimpse of the McDaniels, and of Jim Bob.

The Martinez family finally came out, and he saw Angie drop L.D.'s arm to approach them. Her words were inaudible, but he could catch the lilt of her voice as she spoke to them in Spanish. She embraced the old couple, a compassionate gesture that didn't go unnoticed by Charles. He felt love for her bubbling up, followed by a stab of such jealousy of L.D. that he felt ill. He was unaware of his two deputies watching him.

"Sheriff," Raul's voice tugged him back to reality. "Leon McDaniels looks ready to collapse.''

Charles switched his attention to Leon. The older man looked ravished by grief. The gossips would be speculating for weeks about his behavior. His wife had an expression of distaste, as if she found the funeral a vulgar display of emotion. She grasped Leon's arm as if she were afraid he would escape her. Charles looked more closely at her face and saw the lines of strain that made her appear older, and he felt an unwelcome burst of compassion for her. An unwanted wife, her youth behind her, she was sustained only by her pride. "Meenie, I want to talk to Geneva McDaniels after the funeral. Bring Leon, too, since she probably won't come without him."

His eyes moved on to seek Jim Bob. The usually exuberant man was subdued, almost morose. Charles wondered if the funeral had shaken him enough to make him talk about Saturday night. Without some corroborating evidence, he couldn't charge Jim Bob with murder just because he refused to talk about where he was. The jail wasn't big enough to hold everyone if that were his only criteria. He crammed his Stetson back on his head and headed toward Jim Bob.

"That casket holds the charred bones and flesh of a seventeen-year-old girl. If your actions force me to suspect you when you're innocent, then you're giving tacit approval to the person who killed her. Do you want that kind of animal walking around free? He has successfully murdered twice and attempted it twice more. Do you think he'll stop now? The next time his warped mind senses danger, he'll react the same way. Are you willing to be responsible for someone else's death? Give me a good reason to cross you off my list."

Charles's eloquent plea seemed to shake Jim Bob. He looked at the casket being carried out of the church by the pallbearers, the sun reflecting off its polished surface.

"It could be a member of your family next, Jim Bob," Charles said softly.

Jim Bob pulled a handkerchief out of his breast pocket and wiped his face. He didn't look at Charles, but stared, mesmerized by the casket being lifted into the hearse. "You checked my pickup; that ought to prove I didn't kill anybody."

"Not necessarily. You could have changed the tires."

Jim Bob's eyes took on the look of a cornered animal. "Sheriff, I didn't kill her. Hell, I won't even go hunting. And I didn't change my tires. For God's sake, can't you believe me?" Jim Bob's voice rose, and several people turned to look at him. His eyes darted from side to side, seeking some way out. He licked his lips and wiped his face again. His eyes swung back to Charles, pleading with him to believe.

Charles shook his head. "I can't take your word for it, Jim Bob, not about murder."

Jim Bob took a deep breath and exhaled, the air whistling through his teeth. "I was playing poker," he confessed, and dropped his eyes to study the toes of his boots.

Charles felt a combination of relief and fury—relief that he could definitely cross one suspect off his list, and fury that such a harmless alibi could have wasted so much of his time. His stern features twisted with anger. "Damn you! Wasting my time because you wouldn't tell me you were playing a card game. What in the hell do you think I'm doing, playing a child's game of Clue? I'm looking for a murderer and you hem and haw around about telling me you were playing poker. I hope you lost every last dime you had, you stupid fool!" Charles's voice was tight sounding as he attempted to control his temper.

Jim Bob flinched at Charles's words. "It's not such a little thing, Sheriff. Good God! If you knew my mother-in-law, you'd be afraid to confess to playing poker, too. That old bat'll be after my wife to leave me if she finds out I've been gambling again. Hell, I'm surprised she wasn't out marching around the bingo stand with Miss Poole, except she and Miss Poole don't get along. Sheriff, you got to keep that poker game quiet."

"All right, Jim Bob. I won't tell your mother-in-law if you cooperate from now on. If you get stubborn just once, I'll take her out to dinner and tell her everything I know."

Jim Bob grabbed Charles's hand, jerking it up and down like a man priming a pump. "Sheriff, so help me God, I'll do anything you say. You just tell me what you want, and I'll do it."

"Just tell where and who you played with."

"Anything, Sheriff; anything at all," said Jim Bob enthusiastically. "I played poker at Sammy's place out on 1283. There was me; Red Turner, the airport manager; Russell Gentry, the owner of the spraying service; and a couple of other guys from out of town that I didn't know. Just ask any of them. They'll tell you I was there until three o'clock in the morning.

That's why I was late on Sunday. I had a hell of a hangover and just couldn't get out to the barbecue pit at six o'clock.''

Charles felt his case against Sammy dissolving. "Then Sammy was there?''

Jim Bob considered a moment. "Well, he ran back to town to get some beer about ten o'clock. The cheapskate didn't buy enough. Took him a hell of a long time, too. Said he had a flat tire and had to stop and change it. He sure as hell was dirty when he got back.''

"Did anything else happen that night, Jim Bob?'' Charles asked, his stomach tightening up.

"Well, yeah. Sammy got a phone call about two o'clock or thereabouts. I didn't hear much of that, just his end, and he didn't say much. Told someone he'd meet him at six o'clock. Then he saw me listening, so he took the phone around the corner. I was gonna tell him he better get his lazy butt to the barbecue pit on time, but I was dealt four sevens and forgot. God, that was some hand! I cleaned everybody out that hand.'' Jim Bob's eyes sparkled with the memory.

Charles stuffed his hands in his pockets, knowing if he didn't he would strangle Jim Bob right where he stood. "You damn fool! If you'd told me that when I talked to you the first time, two people wouldn't be in the hospital. Two people were shot because you were worried about protecting your damn hide. Now get down to my office and tell Raul you want to make a statement.''

"You mean Sammy did it, Sheriff?'' Jim Bob's eyes were round in shock.

"Let's say, as the British do, that Sammy is helping me with my inquiries,'' Charles said. "Now beat it, before I change my mind and decide to charge you with illegal gambling.''

Watching Jim Bob scurrying away like an overweight chipmunk, Charles felt a hand on his arm. Turning, he saw Jack Colchester, and smiled. "Well, if it isn't the owner, editor, and star reporter of the *Crawford County Examiner*. Don't tell me you knew Maria, too?''

"No, but Roberto writes a column for the Spanish-language section of the paper. Besides, a good reporter always attends the funerals of murder victims. I'll be going to Billy Joe's this afternoon. Will you be there?''

"No, I'll send someone," Charles said as the two walked toward the parking lot.

"You mean you aren't going to check out the mourners for your murderer?''

"I think I can say with some certainty that I have the murderer safely locked up. But that's not for publication," he added hastily. "I still have a lot of statements to take, and some loose ends to tie up before I can formally charge him with murder.''

"Might I ask, not for publication, of course, just whom you have locked up and on what charge?'' Jack Colcheter asked.

"Sammy, our crooked J.P. And I arrested him for suspicion of accepting a bribe.''

Jack's gaunt cheeks rounded out as he soundlessly whistled. "You finally caught him with his hand under the table. I'm glad about that, but I'm afraid your murder charge will never materialize. I quizzed Jim Bob and discovered he was playing poker at Sammy's house. His mother-in-law was on the warpath about his getting in after four o'clock in the morning. She suspects he was either gambling or out with a woman. I think she prefers adultery to gambling.''

"I know about the poker game; I caught Jim Bob at a weak moment and he finally told me. However, he also told me Sammy left the game at about the right time and was gone for a long while. When he came back, he was dirty and claimed he had changed a flat tire. He also received a phone call at the crucial time, so it looks pretty conclusive.''

"Jim Bob didn't tell me that. He spent most of the time with a minute-by-minute replay of a poker hand.''

"I know," Charles said dryly. "He was dealt four sevens.''

Jack stopped by his car. "He told you, too? You know, Charles, I never had four of a kind in my life. I wonder what it feels like.''

"Now, Jack, gambling is illegal in Texas," the sheriff chided.

"You'd never get a jury in Texas to convict a man for a friendly poker game.''

Charles grinned. "Yes I would. I'd make sure Miss Poole was on the jury."

Jack looked at Charles, amusement in his eyes. "My God, Sheriff, you have a Machiavellian mind. By the way, how are Miss Poole and Old Ben? I'm doing an article on the shootings and putting it right next to the feature on Maria. I take it they're part and parcel of the same case?"

"I think so, unless you choose to believe we have two killers running around loose, and that would be stretching coincidence too far," Charles replied. "And to answer your question, Miss Poole is doing fine. Old Ben is still alive, but he hasn't regained consciousness yet. The doctor wasn't very encouraging when I talked to him this morning. If he does live, maybe he will talk to me when he finds out Sammy is in jail and can't hurt him."

"Did you ever find the gun?"

"No, and I don't know what he did with it. I don't think anyone had a chance to leave that courthouse after the shootings without being seen. Certainly no one could have walked out with a gun. But we'll find it, if I have to tear the building down brick by brick."

"Good luck. I think you're going to need that gun to convict Sammy." Jack slid into his car and waggled his hand at the sheriff.

Walking by the dispatcher toward his office later on, Charles saw Jim Bob by Raul's desk dictating his statement. Raul had a glazed look in his eyes, and Charles wondered if the statement would include a lengthy description of the famous four sevens.

"Sheriff." Charles cringed at the sound of Mabel's nasal voice. "Poor Sammy just couldn't eat that horrible food this morning, so I ordered a special breakfast from the café across the street. I just can't imagine why you arrested him, a respected public official like that."

Charles whirled and slammed his fist on her desk. "Damn it!" he roared. "Sammy gets no more or less than any other prisoner. He can eat the same food as everyone else. And in case you didn't know, Sammy is under arrest for taking a bribe. Respected public officials do not take bribes. From this point on, you tend to your duties as dispatcher, and let the jailer tend to his.'' Charles lowered his voice to a deadly whisper. ''If you ever give a prisoner extra privileges without asking me, I will fire you. Is that understood?''

''Yes,'' Mabel said, sniffing loudly. ''I'm sure it's all a mistake, though.''

''You let me worry about the mistakes around here. That's what I'm paid to do. And you keep your nose out of the jail.''

Charles stomped into his office, anger making white lines around his tightly compressed lips. One way or another, he was going to get rid of Mabel.

Sinking into his chair, he rested his head in his hands, his fingers twisting his hair. Still so much to do to tighten his case against Sammy. Statements from the other poker players, and from Billy Joe's mother, search warrants for each of Sammy's two houses and his airplane hangar, and God only knew what else might be needed at the last minute. Charles checked his watch and decided to see if L.D. was back from the funeral.

''County attorney's office.'' The breathy voice that answered the phone belied the true appearance of its owner. L.D.'s secretary Cathy Underwood was a plump efficient grandmother in her fifties. Charles often teased her about her sexy voice to watch her cheeks turn pink in pleased embarrassment.

''Cathy, is your illustrious boss in the office?''

''Yes, Sheriff; he just came in. He doesn't seem to be in a very good mood.''

''Tell him I'm on the line, will you? I need to talk to him.''

''Just a minute, Sheriff. I'll buzz him.''

''Charles, what do you need?'' L.D.'s voice was edgy, almost impatient.

''Whoa, there. You sound like you want to pick a fight, and I don't have my guns on,'' Charles joked, concerned at the sound of his friend's voice.

''Sorry, Charles, I'm still a little uptight from that funeral. And then Angie had to make a spectacle of herself. That didn't help much either.''

Charles gripped the phone harder. ''I'd have thought you'd

have been proud of her, L.D. She's a very compassionate person."

"Compassion is all right, but hugging those people was carrying things too far. She didn't know Maria that well. Everyone was staring at her."

"I think you're being too critical, or should I say, you're being too much of a damn politician, always worrying about your image."

"All right, Charles! Don't get on your high horse; one of us in a bad mood is enough. I should know better than to criticize Angie in front of you. You spend more time worrying about her than I do."

L.D. sounded amused, and Charles felt guilty. He had to learn to control his knee-jerk reactions to critical comments about her.

"I'm sorry, L.D. I didn't mean to stick my nose in where it doesn't belong," Charles said stiffly, then cursed himself for his stilted voice.

L.D. laughed. "Anytime you do that, I promise I'll pinch it off. Now, what was it you needed?"

"Three search warrants, for Sammy's two houses and his hangar."

"What are you searching for?"

"Further evidence of his taking bribes, such as bank accounts under another name, records, etc. He can't be funneling that money through his own account or the IRS would get suspicious. I also want to check his tires," Charles added.

"You're pushing. You go on a fishing expedition with a search warrant and the district judge will throw out your evidence. Besides, if Angie heard about that cast, you know damn well Sammy did."

"I'm a lawyer, too, L.D. I know how far I can push, and I have reason, good reason, to believe Sammy is guilty of murder." Charles recounted Jim Bob's story.

"My God, it sounds like you got him. Congratulations! I never thought you would ever pin this on anyone!"

Charles was irked by L.D.'s choice of words. "I'm not pinning it on him! I believe he is the murderer. Just hurry those warrants up, will you? I want the county judge to sign them so I can search Sammy's property this afternoon.''

"I'll have Cathy bring them up when they're ready. I just hope you know what you're doing. By the way, how are Miss Poole and Old Ben? Has the old man told you anything yet?''

"Miss Poole is going to be fine, but Old Ben is still unconscious. The doctor gives him less than a fifty-fifty chance. I keep thinking of what he told me in jail when I asked him what was frightening him. He just kept saying he didn't know. I think he saw someone, probably at the barbecue pit, but wasn't able to recognize who it was. I wonder if he is going to be a threat to the murderer at all. It's going to be ironic if Sammy shot two people and got himself caught for no good reason.''

"I never thought of that. I just assumed he must have seen something or someone close enough to identify them. He must have, or else why would he call attention to himself by demanding to be locked up?'' L.D. asked.

Charles shook his head in disagreement, forgetting that L.D. couldn't see him. "I believed that too until I thought about his insistence that he didn't know what was frightening him. No, I think, looking at the whole thing logically, the murderer is safe from anything damaging Old Ben might say.''

"But can the murderer depend on that?'' L.D. asked.

"The question is academic, since he's locked up in jail. It's a good thing, too, because I was beginning to suspect the damnedest people.''

"Like who?'' L.D. asked curiously.

"Leon's wife,'' Charles answered.

L.D. was silent for a moment. "That's not such a bad guess at that.''

"I don't have to worry anymore. I've got the murderer. I'm going back upstairs to wait for the McDaniels and tell them to go back home. It's all over, and you have no idea how relieved I am.''

"Oh, I think I do,'' L.D. said, his good humor restored.

# CHAPTER

# 17

"SHERIFF," SAID MEENIE, THROWING OPEN CHARLIE'S office door, "the McDaniels are here."

Charles hurriedly pulled his feet off his desk and unfolded his long body from his chair. This was going to be enough of a ticklish situation without his being caught with his feet propped on his desk. "Leon, Mrs. McDaniels, please come in."

Leon moved slowly into the room, his face gray under his tan. He lowered himself into a chair as if he had no more strength to stand. His wife followed him, standing behind his chair as if to protect him. Her eyes were fierce as she stared at Charles. "What do you want now? Haven't you done enough? Hounding an innocent man, ruining his reputation. Leave him alone!" Her voice rose, and Charles flinched at its shrill tone.

"Geneva!" Leon's voice cracked, jerking the woman's head around with its command. "Geneva, the sheriff is trying to solve a murder. He had his reasons for suspecting me, and I respect his lack of fear of my position. He was doing what he had to do, and he doesn't need your screaming at him."

"How could he possibly have suspected you. Everyone in the county knew you were following her around like a lovesick puppy. The last thing you'd have done was kill your precious little Maria!"

She circled Leon's chair to brace her hands on Charles's desk. "Don't you know yet she was an ambitious little bitch? She was after my husband, but I sent her on her way. I told her I knew what kind of a girl she was, and to leave him alone or she'd regret it!"

She turned back to kneel at Leon's side. "Don't you see, I

wanted to protect you. I didn't want you to make a fool out of yourself. I didn't want people laughing at you."

Leon looked at her with something akin to pity. "I think the sheriff has heard enough of our personal problems. Why don't you sit down and let's listen to why he wanted to talk to us." Leon shifted his eyes to Charles. "What did you want of us, Sheriff?"

Charles hesitated, his ease with words deserting him. He had meant to merely apologize for this meeting and thank them for coming, but he felt a growing unease. He sighed, and surrendered to his obsession for detail and turned to Geneva McDaniels. "When did you warn Maria to leave your husband alone?"

She raised her head, her face hard and angry. "Saturday afternoon. She came to the house and asked to speak to Leon; she wanted to ask his advice, she said. But I knew better. She was nervous, and she wouldn't look at me. She didn't want advice, she wanted my husband, and she was afraid she would give herself away if she looked at me. I told her to get out, that Leon wasn't home, and she had better not to try to see him alone."

Leon rose in one swift motion and grasped his wife by the shoulders. "Damn you! You didn't even ask her what was wrong, did you? You just condemned her without listening! If you weren't such a cold, hard woman, Maria would be alive today! None of this need have happened!"

Charles came around his desk and grabbed Leon's arm. "Leave her alone. We can't know what Maria might have told you. It might have had nothing to do with her condition."

"What condition?" Leon's wife demanded, rubbing her shoulders where her husband's fingers had dug into the tender flesh.

"Maria was pregnant, and you drove her out to be murdered!" Leon spat out the words.

Geneva leaned back in her chair and laughed, her body shaking with the force of it. Charles stood frozen in place, horrified by her reaction. Leon raised his fist, a terrifying anger twisting his face. He stood over her, his body rigid as he fought an internal battle. Finally he slumped, dropped his arm, and sank back in his chair. "I can't hit her even when I hate her. I've spent too many years protecting her."

Charles leaned against his desk and pressed his hand over his belly where the familiar burning was beginning. "I know, Leon." He stopped to search for words, to admit he too had had a wife he had to protect against herself, but Geneva McDaniels interrupted.

"I'm glad I turned her away. She'd have destroyed my marriage. You'd have taken her in, discarded me like some piece of garbage—and over a baby that couldn't have been yours."

"Maria wouldn't have destroyed our marriage. You managed to do that years ago." Leon walked to the door and left without a backward glance.

"You could've killed her, couldn't you, Mrs. McDaniels? You hated her badly enough," Charles said softly.

Geneva McDaniels raised her head to look at him, her blue eyes glittering with hate. "If I did, it was all for nothing, wasn't it?"

"Yes," he agreed simply.

She picked up her purse and rose, turning back to face him, her hand on the doorknob, her eyes holding a queer kind of triumph. "But if I don't have him, neither does she." She exited, closing the door softly behind her.


"Crawford thirty-two, come in." Charles released the button and braced himself for Mabel's voice.

"Thirty-two, go ahead." Not even distance and technology could filter out the nasal quality of her voice.

"Is Meenie back from Billy Joe's funeral?"

"Yes, Sheriff," Mabel replied.

"Is he there?"

"Yes, Sheriff."

"Well, damn it, let me talk to him!" Charles wondered how Mabel had ever lived to her advanced age.

"Sheriff, profanity over the air is illegal," Mabel said piously.

"Mabel, if you don't tell Meenie I want to talk to him, I promise you more profanity than you can handle."

"Sheriff, what do you need?" Meenie's gruff voice seemed melodious to Charles's ears.

"Come out to the airport, Meenie. We have a couple of searches to do."

Charles hung up his microphone without listening to Meenie sign off and leaned against his patrol car. He had no heart for the search. What if it turned up no further proof? L.D. was right: if anyone had heard about the cast, it would be Sammy. And if they couldn't produce a tire to match it, then the jury would never find the J.P. guilty.

He rubbed his aching temples with thumbs, thinking of Geneva McDaniels. Maria alive would have been less of a threat to her than Maria dead. Whoever murdered the girl had an unwitting accomplice in Leon's wife. Her jealousy had driven a scared teenager to a lonely meeting with death.

The sight of Meenie's car turning onto the gravel road leading to the hangar areas jerked Charles from his depression.

"Sheriff, what are we going to search?" Meenie's cheek was well rounded again with tobacco. He leaned against the open car door and gauged the distance of a sunflower. Shifting his tobacco, he took aim and missed. His mouth dropped open in disbelief. Charles threw back his head and laughed.

"That ain't very kind, Sheriff." Meenie sounded hurt.

Charles slapped Meenie on the back, feeling that he had seen everything; the world held no more surprises. "I'm sorry. I've had a hard day. Then to see you miss a target, I just had to laugh or cry. Since I know crying would ruin my image, I laughed instead. I'm really sorry, Meenie," he repeated. "What went wrong?"

"I ain't had a chew all day, and spittin' is something you have to practice. It's like playing the piano: you just can't take a day away from it. Two funerals in one day just ruined my practice schedule."

"The funerals are over for a while. Who was at Billy Joe's?"

"The editor, and his mother and some of her friends. There were a few young toughs that hung out at the bars with Billy Joe. L.D. and his wife were there. I can't figure out, unless it was because Billy Joe worked for his daddy for a while.

'Course, with these politicians you never know; he mighta been looking for votes, too.''

Meenie shifted his tobacco and spit again, this time hitting the sunflower square in the center.

"L.D. is a friend of mine, Meenie," Charles said coldly. "And I don't think his political ambitions carry him as far as to solicit votes at a funeral."

"Sorry, Sheriff. I don't mean to run down your friends." Meenie sounded singularly unrepentent. "His wife sure is a nice lady."

"Yes, she is," Charles agreed, quickly turning his head to look down the runway. "Let's get this search over with, Meenie. I don't know if we're going to find anything or not." He pulled the warrant out and headed toward Sammy's hangar.

Meenie trotted along behind Charles, his shorter legs taking quick steps to keep up with the taller man. "I read Jim Bob's statement, and it sounds like you got Sammy dead to rights."

Charles slid the sheet-metal hangar door rattling along its tracks to let the sun light up the interior. A small tool chest was the only thing in the concrete-floored hangar besides a small two-engine plane.

"I don't know anymore, Meenie. Every time I think I've got the case solved, something else happens and I find myself back at the beginning. Take the plane, and I'll take the tool chest."

After looking through the splintered wooden chest, Charles climbed to his feet and wiped his hands on his handkerchief. Kicking the lid shut in disgust, he walked over to the plane. "Did you find anything?" he asked Meenie.

"Nothin' in the plane itself, but his log is kinda interesting. He sure put a lot of hours on the engine. Look here." Meenie's stubby, gnarled finger traced the entries in the pilot's log. "He made a long trip about once a month. From the hours, I figure he must'a been near the border. I could be wrong, though; he coulda gone north or west."

"I think you were right the first time. I've been keeping a close eye on Sammy's jaunts, out of idle curiosity. He's got quite a little arrest record in Dallas and El Paso."

"Do you think he's running wetbacks?"

Charles shuddered at the image of illegal aliens in the hands of Sammy. "I don't think this plane is big enough to make it profitable. He could be a broker of some kind, though, acting as a go-between for people who need cheap labor. It's more likely he just wanted to sample the fleshpots of the larger cities. Take the log anyway, Meenie. We can always turn it over to the border patrol. Let's go over to his place on 1283 where the big poker game took place. Maybe he's got some records—bank statements or something—hidden there. I'll follow you, since I don't know which cattle guard to turn at."

Meenie shook his head and spat on the concrete floor. "I don't know how a city boy like you ever got elected sheriff."

Charles grinned crookedly, his features smoothing out to appear almost boyish. "It's my charm, Meenie. That and the fact the voters were enamored of the idea of an attorney being sheriff. Don't tell me you hold my background against me?"

"Hell, no, Sheriff. I voted for you, but charm didn't have nothin' to do with it. I just thought it was time we had an honest man in office, instead of a good ol' boy. I always know where I stand with you, and so does everybody else. You're a fair man, even if you can't tell the difference between maize and wheat. I bet you can't even ride a horse."

"I can ride a horse, but not very well. And I don't think I could compete with the cowboys around here."

Meenie shifted his wad and took aim at a fly on the hangar wall. "Nobody can compete with a real cowboy, sheriff. They're born to the saddle."

"Get in the car and lead on, Meenie. I'm anxious to get this over with one way or another."

He followed Meenie's car as it turned on the state highway for a few hundred feet before turning south on 1283. The hot sun and intermittent gusts of wind were similar to Sunday's weather.

Charles followed Meenie onto a dirt road, grain crops on either side. The dust raised by their two cars hung in pale tan clouds along the dirt road to the old white frame house.

"Sammy's grandparents built this place. His parents lived here all their lives. They were good people; don't know how they ended up with Sammy." Meenie's voice was low, as if he felt the sacrilege Sammy had brought upon his family.

"Let's do it, Meenie," Charles said. He tried the front door, to find it locked.

"That's a little funny," Meenie said. "Most folks don't lock their doors around here."

He crouched down to examine the lock, then whistled. "That's a dead bolt. Now why did Sammy think he needed a dead bolt on this old place. He doesn't live out here. There couldn't be much worth stealin'."

"I brought his key ring. Maybe I'll be lucky and one of these will fit." Charles looked at the keys and picked out one. He grinned as it slid smoothly into the lock. Pushing open the door, he and Meenie entered the hot, stuffy house. Sammy had evidently not bothered to replace any of the old furniture from the days of his parents and grandparents. The only modern piece was a television set sitting in one corner. A round oak dining table still held cards and dirty glasses from the famous poker game. A telephone stood on a small table by the door. Musty floral carpets covered most of the floors, except the kitchen, which had linoleum at least thirty years old. Charles could see an old iron bedstead in a bedroom that opened off the living room.

"I don't know about you, but I feel as if I'm disturbing the dead," Charles said, his voice seeming to echo in the old house.

Meenie nodded his agreement. "Sammy's ma and pa would sure be upset by what he's done."

The two men methodically began searching the living room, opening each drawer of an old desk, picking up cushions, and removing and checking each volume in an old bookcase. Defeated, they moved on to the dining room to search a china cabinet.

"He surely didn't bother to keep this place clean," said Charles, wiping his finger across the surface of an old sideboard.

"It's kind of hard to do on the farm," Meenie replied. "The dirt from the fields blows in faster than you can clean it out. He coulda washed his dishes, though. The cockroaches are thicker than fleas on a dog."

Meenie started to search the kitchen, pulling open the old

drawers, the enamel paint chipped and peeling. He got down on his hands and knees to peer under the sink. "Bunch of sacks of something under here," he said, reaching to pull one out.

Charles turned sharply, his search of the top cabinets forgotten. He watched Meenie stack three small plastic bags on the counter top. His hands trembling, he opened one and, wetting a forefinger, touched it to the white powder and tasted a minute amount. Turning his head, he spat violently. Wiping his handkerchief across his mouth, he looked into Meenie's eyes. "It's cocaine," he whispered.

"Good God! That's enough to keep the whole Panhandle, including the cows, on a high for months," Meenie said, his usual imperturbable calm deserting him.

"He must be a distributor of some kind. There's too much here for him to be just a pusher." He looked at the cocaine again, an innocent-looking powder that represented so much wealth and untold misery. "This is why he made those monthly trips to the border: he had to pick up more of this poison. Lists. There have to lists of some kind. Surely he can't remember the names of all his pushers. Somewhere he has a record of names, or at least phone numbers of his contacts. The narcotic boys are going to love this."

"Couldn't happen to a nicer guy, Sheriff. But it sure does give a kick in the head to your murder case."

Charles rubbed his chin thoughtfully. "Not necessarily, Meenie. It may just be we've been looking at this thing from the wrong angle. Maybe Maria knew about the drugs and tried a little blackmail. Maybe the pregnancy had nothing to do with the motive."

"That would make more sense than believing she was sleeping with that snake."

"Don't libel snakes; some of them are useful," the sheriff chided.

"I never liked nothin' that crawled on its belly."

"That description fits Sammy," Charles agreed. "Now, let's see what else we can find."

The heat grew more oppressive as they searched the last bedroom. Dingy sheets covered the bed, and a few clothes hung in the closet. "Sammy must have slept here," Meenie said. "It stinks just like him."

Charles grunted in agreement as he pulled out a dresser drawer and turned it over. "This is it, Meenie," he said quietly, pointing to a cheap spiral notebook taped to the bottom of the drawer. Peeling up the tape with one fingernail, he let it drop to the floor. Using his pocket knife, he flipped open the pages. Names and phone numbers seemed to jump from the page. Meenie knelt down to look over his shoulder.

"Some of them numbers are in Amarillo; I recognize the prefixes. And look there, Sheriff: there's abbreviations out to the side."

" 'AMR' stands for Amarillo, Meenie. And this set of letters is for Denver," said Charles, slipping a ballpoint pen through the spiral. "Let's get this back to the office. After you fingerprint it, we can read it at our leisure before we call in the Department of Public Safety and the Justice Department. I've jurisdiction over Crawford County, so I personally am going to arrest the hometown pushers. Grab the cocaine, and let's get out of here."

Meenie headed back to the kitchen, skirting the dining table with its scattered cards and overflowing ashtrays. He stopped for a minute and pulled a crumbled piece of paper out of one of the ashtrays. "Sheriff, did you look at this table?" he asked after unfolding the paper.

"No," Charles said, stopping by Meenie's elbow. "I didn't think I would find any lists written on a card."

Meenie stretched his hand out, the note held between two fingers. "I'm sorry, Sheriff."

Charles looked numbly at the paper. The name was not familiar, but the time scrawled below it was.

Sammy had met someone at six o'clock, but it wasn't Billy Joe Williams.

# CHAPTER

# 18

"DAMN IT, SLIM, GET ME A CUP OF COFFEE!" CHARLES shouted through his closed office door. He rubbed his face, feeling a stubble just under the point of his chin where he had missed shaving. His return to the courthouse with reasonable proof that Sammy had not committed the murders had kept him in his office until past the midnight shift change. Rubbing his eyes with the heels of his hands, he looked again at the stack of statements taken the day Maria's body was uncovered. He had read and reread them until his burning eyes had forced him home to sleep. Somewhere in all that paper was a clue to a murderer.

"Sheriff?" Mabel's voice grated in his ears like fingernails on a blackboard. He could almost feel the hair on the back of his neck stiffening. "Sheriff, Slim isn't here this morning. He's at the hospital on guard duty."

"I forgot about that, Mabel." Charles forced his eyes to focus. "Where's my coffee?"

"Slim always makes the coffee, and he's not here."

"I don't give a damn if Peter Rabbit always makes the coffee. You and whoever else is out there can flip a coin, but somebody had better get me a cup of coffee fast. If I don't get my coffee, Mabel, do you know what I'm going to do?" At her headshake, he got out of his chair and advanced on her, his teeth bared and fingers curled into talons. "I'm personally going to make coyote bait out of everybody in this department. I'm going to strip the hide off everyone and make jerky out of it. Now, if you happen to like your hide in one piece instead of strips, you'll get your butt back there and make some coffee."

Mabel squealed and jumped, bumping into the sheriff's

spitoon and sending it spinning against the wall. She rushed through the door, past her dispatcher's desk, and down the stairs to the second floor ladies room. Charles brushed imaginary lint from his shirt and strolled to the door. Raul and Meenie stood in the outer room, gaping at the departing Mabel.

Meenie grinned, shifting his tobacco to the other cheek. "What'd you do to Mabel, Sheriff? She tore out of here like she had a bear on her tail."

"We merely had a discussion about the proper division of duties," Charles said airily. "Come in here, you two. I need to talk."

The two deputies followed him into his office, Meenie retrieving the forgotten spitoon. Charles sank into his chair and propped his feet on his desk. He had better enjoy being sheriff while it lasted, because when he admitted he couldn't catch a murderer, the voters would very likely kick him out the next election. He wondered what ex-sheriffs did. Sit around like ex-Presidents and write their memoirs? He jerked upright, his feet hitting the floor with a thud, and slammed his fist on the desk. "Damn it! *I will catch that killer!*"

"We're behind you, Sheriff. Just tell us what to do," said Raul softly.

"That's just it, Raul: I don't know what to do. I thought I had Sammy dead to rights, caught with parathion on his hands. Instead, I break up a three-state drug ring. Jim Bob's got a solid gold alibi, and Leon couldn't have fathered Maria's child." Picking up the statements, he placed them in the center of the desk, carefully aligning the edges. "I started out with this many people and seem to have ended up empty-handed."

"Somebody's lying or something's been overlooked," Meenie said, leaning over in his chair to aim at the spitoon.

"I know that, Meenie, and what's been overlooked is a closer look at motive. Who involved in this case hated Maria enough to kill her?"

Raul looked sick. "Leon's wife," he whispered.

"And who is the only person who might kill to protect her? The only one who was desperate to know who Miss Poole accused?"

Even Meenie's cynicism was shaken. "Leon McDaniels."

Charles turned his head impatiently when he heard the knock
on the door. "Come in, Mabel. I hope you have the coffee."
His voice died when he saw Slim's earnest face. He didn't
remember getting to his feet, nor did he remember hearing the
crash as his chair toppled over. "What are you doing here?"
he shouted.

"You called the hospital and told me to get on over, so here
I am," Slim answered, puzzled by Charles's actions.

"Who is guarding Old Ben?" Charles asked, feeling nauseous.

"No one, Sheriff. You never said anything about any guard.
Hey, what's going on around here anyway?"

Charles pushed Slim to one side, and ran through the door.
"Call the hospital! Somebody's going to kill Old Ben!" he
shouted at a deputy. He headed for the stairs, followed by Raul
and Meenie.

"You mean the message was a fake?" Slim yelled stum-
bling after them.

"Shut your mouth, boy, and keep runnin'," Meenie panted.
His bowed legs took the stairs three at a time.

The heavy glass doors were slammed against the side of the
foyer as Charles burst through them, his stomach burning with
acid. He jerked open the door of the patrol car and started the
engine and siren. Screeching tires spun gravel as he backed up
and Meenie and Raul threw themselves into the rear seat as the
car took off, its rear door swinging open. Charles's steady
cursing was a background noise to the shrill siren. Slim chased
the car, waving his arms and screaming until giving up, he
jumped into another patrol car and followed, his face so white
his freckles looked like specks of chocolate.

The two cars spun into the emergency parking lot, and
Charles dashed for the door. For the first time since his election
he held his revolver in his hand and knew he wouldn't hesitate
to use it. He heard the sobs over the heavy thudding sound of
his boots before he burst around the corner into the Intensive
Care wing. A nurse was sitting on the floor, her crisp white hat
clutched in her hands. Two other nurses were attempting to
move her, but she pushed at their hands, curling herself up
against the wall. A jagged wound near the hairline was bleed-

ing, covering one side of her face with an obscene red color. One of the nurses placed a pad on it, but her hand was slapped away.

Charles grasped the hysterical woman under the arms and pulled her up. Quickly shifting his hands under her body, he lifted her into his arms. The older of the two nurses pointed to a room and he carried the injured woman in, laying her gently on the bed. "How's Old Ben?" he asked tersely, glancing back across the hall to see Raul take a position in front of the Intensive Care Unit.

"He's all right," answered the older nurse. "I checked on him the minute I found Brenda."

"Where's the doctor?" Charles demanded.

"I've called him. He's coming."

Motioning to the older woman, Charles went back into the hall. "Now what happened here"—he glanced at her badge—"Mrs. Myers?"

"Brenda was on duty in ICU. The monitors are in a little room right next door. There's a glass window between the two rooms so the nurse can see the patient as well as watch the monitoring screens. A call came from you for the deputy to report in as quickly as possible. I relayed the message to Brenda, and not five minutes later I heard her scream. I ran to find out what was wrong and found her lying in the doorway into ICU. I called for another nurse, and quickly checked the patient. He was fine, but his pillow was on the floor. I made him comfortable, called for still another girl to watch the monitors, and Mrs. Atchely and myself tried to help Brenda. We got her as far as the hallway, but she was so terrified, we couldn't persuade her to move any farther."

"Did you see anyone in the hall after you heard Brenda scream?" Charles asked.

"I didn't see anyone, but I had the feeling someone had just left. Do you understand, Sheriff? I can't explain it." Mrs. Myers looked helplessly at Charles, impatient with her own inability.

"I know what you mean," Charles said. "But you didn't actually see anyone?"

"No, but I know I missed him by only a few seconds."

"Meenie, take Slim, and search the hospital. Everybody had better have a damn good reason for being here."

"Sheriff," Mrs. Myers objected, "I can't let you just barge into the rooms. This is a hospital; there are some very ill people here."

"Then you'll have to go with them. But this is as close as we have been to the murderer, and I don't want him getting away."

He turned to Raul. "Don't let anybody in this room. If I want you, I'll send a replacement."

"Don't be too hard on Slim, Sheriff. He's just a kid," Raul said.

"He's going to have to grow up quickly, or find another job. I can't trust kids with people's lives. Now where the hell is that doctor?"

Charles paced, his boots echoing in the long hall. By the time Dr. Wallace rounded the corner, his stethoscope neatly tucked into a pocket of his white coat, Charles's tension was evident in the rigid cast of his muscles and the deep grooves around his mouth. He grabbed the doctor's arm. "I have to talk to that nurse, so don't knock her out," he ordered.

"Listen, young man, this isn't the courthouse, and what you want counts for very little. I will treat that young lady in whatever way I find necessary." Dr. Wallace was bristling.

"Doctor, that nurse saw the murderer; that means she'll have to die, too. The only chance I have of saving her life is to find out what she saw. This man has no compunction against killing. If he had a conscious feeling of guilt, it's gone now. Each murder will become a little easier until he reaches that point where human life means less than a mosquito's."

Dr. Wallace looked shaken. He knew determination when he saw it; he also recognized necessity. "All right, Sheriff. Do what you have to do. God knows I don't want to see any more bullet wounds, or be called to treat a nurse who has been assaulted. I thought Carroll was such a peaceful little town. No violent crime, I told my wife; we won't have to lock ourselves in at night. My God, was I ever wrong! Go on in, and I'll see if I can settle her down long enough to be questioned."

Following the doctor into the room, Charles watched as he

cleaned the girl's wound, carrying on a soothing monologue as he worked, calming the young nurse's hysteria. By the time he finished, Brenda's sobs were intermittent, and her reaction to the assault was beginning to lessen.

At the doctor's gesture, Charles stepped closer to the bed, taking the nurse's hand in his own. "Brenda, I'm Sheriff Matthews. Are you feeling better now?"

Brenda nodded, her face and lips still white. The other nurse covered her with a blanket, tucking it under her chin. "I was so scared." She drew a breath, then clenched her teeth, fighting for composure. "It was awful."

"I know it was," said Charles sympathetically. "I hate having to ask you to recall the incident, but I must. You realize that, don't you? You know it can't wait?"

"Yes," she whispered.

"Take your time, and tell me everything that happened," Charles said, hooking a chair leg with the toe of his boot. Pulling it close to the bed, he sat down and folded Brenda's hand in both of his. At first it lay limp between his palms, then she clutched his hand tighter and tighter with her own, as if his touch was a lifeline protecting her from her recollection of the past.

"I was watching the monitors, occasionally looking at the patient, when Mrs. Myers buzzed me on the intercom to tell me to give the deputy your message. I told him, and he seemed unsure about whether to leave. When he finally left, I went back to check the screens. Everything seemed perfectly all right. Then I looked up to see a doctor enter the room. He was in scrub clothes, even had his face mask up. I thought that was funny. No one ever leaves those masks on outside surgery; they're too hot. I thought maybe it was Dr. Wallace—I mean, I never expected anyone else to wear a scrub suit. I knew you thought the old man was in danger, but I never really believed it."

"When did you realize it wasn't Dr. Wallace?" Charles asked.

"When I saw him pull the pillow from under the patient's head and hold it over his face. I must have yelled—I don't remember, I don't remember. Anyway, the man jerked around.

I didn't call for help; all I could think of was saving that poor old man. I ran into the room, and I remember those eyes, and seeing the metal pitcher in his hand. I think I screamed. I woke up in the hall, and I was so scared, I didn't want anyone to touch me." Brenda lay silently, tears running from the corners of her eyes to wet her pillow.

Dr. Wallace touched Charles' shoulder. "Do you need to ask anything else?"

"Brenda, did you recognize the man?" Charles asked urgently.

She shook her head. "But I won't forget those eyes. They were blue and seemed to shoot sparks at me. I couldn't see the rest of his face. The surgical hat and mask hid everything. I couldn't even see his ears."

"Okay, Brenda, I understand. Do you think you would recognize his eyes if you saw them again?"

"I don't know. I mean, there wasn't anything special about them except the expression."

"What about his eyebrows, Brenda, what color were they? Were they thick or thin? Was he tall or short? Fat or thin?"

Brenda smiled shyly. "I never thought about his eyebrows. They were sort of sandy colored, and he was taller than me. And he wasn't fat," she added.

Charles stood up, squaring his shoulders. "Was he as tall as me?"

"No," said Brenda, frowning a little. "But then you're pretty tall, aren't you?"

"Six three," Charles replied. "Was the person shorter than the doctor?"

Brenda shook her head hopelessly. "I don't think so. But it's hard to say, Sheriff; he seemed so big when he came at me with that pitcher."

"Are you sure it was a man, Brenda?" he asked suddenly.

The young woman looked confused for a moment. "I think so. I mean, I had the impression it was a man."

Charles leaned closer. "But you were expecting it to be a man, weren't you?"

"Yes," she said hesitantly, "but I'm just sure it was a man. It just had to be. A woman couldn't be as violent as that."

Charles thought of Geneva McDaniels' hate-filled eyes. Some women had the capacity for violence. "You've helped a lot, Brenda. Tomorrow one of my deputies will take your statement." Charles disengaged his hand and flexed his fingers. That girl had a hell of a grip. "Doctor, is Old Ben conscious?"

"No, and I'm not going to try to wake him up. Miss Poole is conscious—a little woozy, but conscious. She isn't too coherent, and it is making her furious."

Charles ran his fingers through his hair as he realized that he hadn't given a thought to Miss Poole. Knowing she had no information to impart, he simply had forgotten her. A shudder rippled his frame. No attempt had been made to kill her, only Old Ben. And only one suspect knew she had no knowledge of the murderer's identity: Leon McDaniels.

Charles nodded at the doctor and, leaning down, patted Brenda's shoulder. "Goodbye, Brenda." He closed the door and walked down the hall.

The hospital was built in the shape of a capital E, with the emergency room in one wing, the nurses' station in the center across from the surgical wing, and the Intensive Care Unit housed in the top wing along with a private suite, supply rooms, and an emergency exit. It was an ideal place for a murder, completely isolated from the nurses' station. Anyone could enter from the emergency door and go down the hall and into ICU without being seen.

Charles caught up with Meenie in the hall by the nurses' station. "Have you found anything?"

"A scrub suit, including a face mask and a pair of surgical gloves, in a broom closet next to ICU. I figure he stripped it off and ducked out the back door. Hell, no one saw him. The nurses were trying to calm the young woman and weren't looking at the back door. The next wing is surgery and there ain't no windows. We questioned everyone in all the rooms, and no one saw anybody."

Charles kneaded the back of his neck where tension had tightened muscles into knots. "I can't believe the chances this man is taking. He could have been caught this morning so easily. He could have been seen entering the surgery to steal the scrub suit. The nurse could have ducked, or pulled the face mask down. Any number of things could have happened. He's had the devil's own luck so far.''

Meenie shifted his tobacco and pursed his lips. "I called out the rest of the deputies and the city cops. We had this place sealed up pretty fast. I think he was gone before we even got here. He's gonna push his luck too far one of these days."

"What bothers me is we may be knee deep in bodies before that happens," Charles said. "I'm going to visit Miss Poole." He looked around, a puzzled frown ceasing his forehead. "Where's Slim?"

"I sent him back to ICU. I figured he's learned his lesson."

"You're overstepping the bounds, Meenie. I'm the one to assign guards, and I can't trust him." Anger caused little furrows to appear in his forehead.

"That's up to you, Sheriff. You're the boss, and I ain't meanin' to step on your toes. I think he did a lot of growin' up today. I also told him he better not move his butt outa that doorway unless you personally looked him in the eye and told him to leave."

"You think that's sufficient?"

"Hell, Sheriff, what else you goin' to do? We ain't got a lot of manpower, and you need Raul and me to take statements. Slim damn sure can't do that. Besides, Raul ain't goin' to leave it to Slim until you tell him it's all right."

Charles reached unconsciously for his hat before he remembered he hadn't taken time to put it on. "You're right, of course, Meenie. I've got to make do with what I've got. But I damn sure don't have to like it." He abruptly turned and walked down the hall.

He knew which room was Miss Poole's by the sight of the city policeman sitting in front of the door. The man got to his feet as Charles walked up. "Sheriff, I'm Patrolman Taylor. No problem here. The old lady is awake off and on. Are you going to talk to her?"

"Yes, I am, Taylor. You can take a ten-minute break. You heard what happened?"

"Yeah," Taylor said grimly. "You don't have to worry

about me. My mama didn't raise no fools. I'm not leaving this
door until you tell me face-to-face."

Charles wondered if Taylor would consider working for the
Sheriff's Department instead of the police.

He pushed open the door and saw Miss Poole, her gray hair
loose about her head. Without the severe hairdo, she appeared
younger and more vulnerable. He touched her hand. "Miss
Poole," he said softly. "It's Sheriff Matthews," he added
quickly when her eyes flew open and she made a frightened
move.

"Sheriff?" she asked uncertainly, blinking her eyes as if to
focus.

"Yes," he said soothingly.

She closed her eyes again. "I was a very stupid old woman.
You were right: real life was more dangerous than my mystery
novels." She moved gingerly, wincing slightly. "That young
doctor told me I had been shot," she said, referring to Dr.
Wallace, who had to be close to fifty. Charles wondered what
Miss Poole's definition of old was. "He wasn't very good, was
he, Sheriff?" Miss Poole asked, a trace of a smile on her face.

For a moment Charles had difficulty following her question
until he realized she was referring to the murderer, rather than
the doctor. "No, he wasn't a very good shot."

Miss Poole smiled again. "I'm glad," she whispered.

He grinned. "I am, too, Miss Poole."

"I think I remember someone whispering about another victim. Who else was shot?"

"Old Ben," Charles replied. "Unfortunately, he was critically injured. Dr. Wallace doesn't know whether he will live."

"Why did they shoot Old Ben? Did he open his mouth when
he should have kept it closed?"

"Just the opposite. He wouldn't tell me anything, so I had
to let him out of jail. Next time I'll follow my intuition instead
of logic."

"Sometimes that's a good idea," Miss Poole said, the
schoolteacher in her surfacing. "Logic quite often fails to take
human nature into account. So who shot me, Sheriff?" she
asked, her blue eyes alert, though still shadowed with pain.

"I don't know, Miss Poole," Charles admitted, running his long fingers through his hair in a gesture of uncertainty. "You dropped your little bombshell of a statement in front of my three suspects. All three of them were in the courthouse at the time of the shooting, but I've no direct evidence against any of them."

Miss Poole seemed puzzled, and she closed her eyes for a moment. "Something's wrong."

"What are you thinking, Miss Poole?" Charles asked uneasily. He didn't want her making any more statements or assumptions about the murder. One instance of Miss Poole acting as a catalyst was enough.

"I'm trying to remember something, Sheriff. Oh dear, it's not fair to be old and drugged, too. My mind keeps skittering about."

"Sheriff!" Meenie's voice seemed to echo in the quiet little room. "Old Ben's awake!"

# CHAPTER
# 19

CHARLES STEPPED INTO ICU TO FIND DR. WALLACE
leaning over Old Ben. "Can I question him?"

The doctor glanced over his shoulder. "Yes, I think so. Just
remember he's in a lot of pain and might have difficulty forming his words. I'll give you a few minutes, but I'm staying. I
won't risk losing him."

"If I don't find out what he knows, you lose him anyway.
The murderer will try again."

"Just remember, when I say leave, that's it," repeated the
doctor, stepping to the other side of the bed and folding his
arms. Charles was reminded of a bodyguard he had once met
in Dallas. He suspected the doctor would prove to be just as
implacable.

"Ben," Charles said softly, leaning over the bed. The old
man's eyes blinked for a moment, mirroring awareness, then
fear. His eyes closed tightly, and he turned his head to burrow
into the pillow. Charles squeezed the old man's hand gently.
"Ben, it's the sheriff. You've been shot."

Old Ben's eyes opened wide. "He tried to kill me. I never
did anything."

"Ben, he tried to kill you again a few minutes ago. And
your nurse stopped him, so he hurt her."

"She was so young." Ben whispered, his voice rusty and
weak. "It wasn't nice, what he did to her."

Wherever Ben was, whatever he was seeing, it was horrifying. His stubbled face grew whiter, beads of sweat forming
a greasy film on his forehead. Dr. Wallace leaned over to take
his pulse.

161

"His pulse is too fast, Sheriff. I'm going to call a stop to the questions. I can't risk a heart attack."

"Doctor, it's not because of my questions. He's remembering something, and he would remember whether I'm here or not. Let him talk, for God's sake. He'll feel better if he does."

"All right, Sheriff. But if his heart starts acting up, you'll have to leave."

Charles didn't waste words arguing. "Ben, what did he do to the young girl? Tell me, Ben." His voice was soft and coaxing, his frustration hidden by a tremendous act of will.

Old Ben lay quietly, his eyes tightly shut. Seconds ticked by in slow motion. The room was quiet, the two men waiting by the bed exchanged glances. Dr. Wallace straightened briskly, shaking his head. "I'm afraid that's all for today, Sheriff. These spells of consciousness will be intermittent. I'm sorry you didn't learn more, but I'll have to ask you to leave now. He's sleeping again."

Charles opened his mouth to object, to beg if necessary, when Ben's weak voice continued as if there had been no interruption. His eyes opened, and he looked at Charles. "He dropped her on the ground. She was hurt bad, because she never moved. I wanted to help her, but I was scared. I didn't want to be hurt." His voice trailed off again.

"You saw the murderer, Ben? Who was it? Tell me so I can stop him from hurting other young girls." Charles waited, scarcely breathing.

"Hurt," Ben moaned. "I hurt so bad. He didn't have to hurt me. Old Ben is a coward."

Charles clenched his fist. "Ben, he'll hurt you again; he'll hurt the young nurse. I have to know who you saw."

"I don't know. It was dark. He put her in the pit and covered her up with something. Then put wood on top of her. It wasn't very nice to bury someone that way."

"What did he do then, Ben?" Charles asked, his stomach burning so badly he was nauseous.

"Got in his pickup," the old man whispered, his grip on Charles's hand surprisingly strong. "My dog barked and ran to the pickup. I hid, I was so scared. Old Ben is such a coward. I never tried to help that poor little girl." He closed his eyes again, but tears seeped between the eyelids and ran down his sunken cheeks.

"Ben, you can help the little girl now," Charles urged. "Tell me what the man looked like. You must avenge her death," he added dramatically.

"It was dark. No headlights on. He wasn't tall as you. Had on a hat. I was behind the pickup, hiding behind some sagebrush. Only saw his back when he climbed in and the light came on."

"What kind of pickup was it?" Charles asked. "Could you tell what color, what make it was?"

Old Ben closed his eyes again, and Charles noticed how transparent the eyelids were. He felt the frail fingers gripping his own. Catching a murderer depended on a badly injured old man who might not live to testify in a trial. Even if he did, he would make a very bad witness.

"BZ-3," Old Ben said in a clear voice, his eyes snapping open.

"What?" Charles asked, momentarily startled.

"I saw the numbers, but I can't remember them all."

"You mean the license plate? You saw the license plate?" Charles asked jubilantly.

"Yes, when he turned the headlights on. BZ-3. I can't remember the rest." He closed his eyes again.

"You're not useless, Ben. I can find out who owns the pickup. You'll save the nurse's life and your own." Charles released Ben's hand, placing it gently on the bed.

"It was a Ford pickup," Ben said suddenly. "I saw the big letters on the tailgate. He killed my little dog. He threw something at it and hit it in the head. He's bad. He picked up whatever hit my dog and then he kicked a poor hurt animal."

Charles had wondered where Old Ben's dog was, but had been too preoccupied to ask. It was just another instance of something being not quite right that he hadn't followed up on. How many other mistakes had he made?

Charles patted Old Ben's hand and straightened, feeling as old and almost as much of a failure as the man in the bed. "Go to sleep, Ben. I'll catch the man so he'll never do bad things again." He glanced at the doctor. "Take good care of him. He doesn't deserve to die because of my stupidity."

Dr. Wallace checked Old Ben's pulse, then tucked the sheets around the old man. He followed Charles out the door, and touched his arm. "Sheriff, I'm going to tell you something a very old doctor told me. 'Sonny,' he said, 'you aren't God. You can do the best a man can do, but God is the only one who doesn't make mistakes.' That old doctor was right. I've spent a lot of time feeling remorse over the years, but I haven't wasted any in self-pity. Now I suggest you do the same."

Charles grasped the doctor's hand. "Thank you," he said.

He gestured to Raul and Meenie to follow him. "Don't even think about leaving this door," he said to Slim.

"I won't, Sheriff, not unless you come tell me in person," Slim said earnestly. Charles had the uncomfortable feeling he was about to cross his heart and hope to die.

"Fine!" Charles said, and headed down the hall with Raul and Meenie as silent companions.

The three men climbed into the patrol car, and Charles put it in reverse, tires screeching in the gravel of the parking lot. He flipped on the siren and drove back to the courthouse, motioning Raul and Meenie to silence when they attempted to question him. "Wait!" he said tersely, concentrating on reaching his office in the shortest possible time. Skidding into his parking place, he bolted out of the car, threw open the courthouse doors, and took the stairs three at a time.

Striding past the dispatcher's desk, Charles headed for the computer with its teletype printer. He consulted a notebook, then typed in the access code to the Department of Safety computer in Austin. Meenie and Raul stood behind him and watched the CRT screen.

"Well, I'll be damned!" Meenie said as he read the query that appeared on the screen. "All pickups registered in Crawford County with license tags beginning with BZ-3." He shifted his tobacco and aimed for a spitoon by the corner of a desk. "So Old Ben did see something. This is it, Sheriff. Can't be too many pickups with the same three numbers."

"I hope not. And I hope it doesn't turn out that it was stolen and never reported." Charles moved over to the teletype printer. He stuck his balled fists into his pockets, wishing for the second time in this case that he hadn't quit smoking. He pulled his hands out of his pockets and ran his fingers through his hair, creating furrows in the crisp, tobacco-colored waves.

The loud click-clack sound of the teletype startled him. He refused to look at the list of names. When the printer stopped, he tore the paper out and walked into his office, Raul and Meenie following him. Sinking into his chair, he spread the list out. He had spent so many hours in this office, reading statements and questioning suspects. It was only fitting he be here for the final resolution.

There were only five lines on the page. Rapidly he ran his finger down the list. Only two Fords were mentioned. He grasped the edge of his desk as he felt shock radiate from his belly outward. His vision blurred momentarily, and he wondered if he might lose consciousness. God knew, he wanted to be unconscious. He wanted to crumble the teletyped sheet into a tiny ball and destroy it.

"Sheriff, what's wrong?" Raul's voice was concerned, its lilt more pronounced. He took the sheet Charles wordlessly passed over to him, and he and Meenie looked at it.

Meenie cleared his throat and aimed a stream of tobacco juice at the spitoon. "You want Raul and me to do it?"

The buzzing phone was a welcome distraction. Charles picked it up, glad of any excuse, no matter how weak, to delay the confrontation with the murderer. "Sheriff Matthews," he said, striving for control of his voice and his emotions.

"Sheriff, this is Miss Poole." Her voice was weak, but had lost none of its certainty. "You were wrong when you said three people overheard my statement at the hamburger stand."

"I know, Miss Poole, but we'll have to talk about it later. I have to arrest a murderer."

"I do wish this case could end poetically, with justice done and the innocent protected."

"There's not much poetic about murder, Miss Poole. Goodbye, now."

Charles hung up without waiting to hear her farewell. He reached into his desk drawer and shook several antacid pills into his hand. He wished they were tranquilizers instead—anything to blur the reality he was about to face.

"Sheriff," Raul said hesitantly. "I think Meenie and I ought to make the arrest."

"No! I have to do it. I have to know why."

"Sheriff," Meenie said, "I ain't always good with words, but I hope you understand what I'm trying to say. There ain't no excuse for this murder. He was guilty of sleeping around and got a girl pregnant. He ought to have faced up to it, took responsibility. If what folks think of you is so important you got to kill to keep in their good graces, then there's something wrong. A man ought to think well of himself by doin' what's decent."

Charles rose and walked to his filing cabinet. He picked up his Stetson and carefully placed it on his head, the ritual comforting, and turned back to the two deputies.

"I understand what you're trying to say, Meenie, but you're wrong. He must have been afraid when he killed Maria. He must have been facing some stress we aren't aware of." Charles pulled open the door and walked through.

"I reckon Raul and me'll just go along with you, Sheriff. Oh, we'll stand back while you do the arresting, but you know its against procedure to arrest a suspect by yourself."

"I can handle it myself," Charles snapped, pushing the elevator. "He won't hurt me."

"I bet that's what Maria thought, too," Meenie said. "Let's just put it this way, Sheriff: we just happen to be going the same way even if you fire us."

"All right, damn it!" Charles said angrily. "But stay out of the way. I don't want him thinking I needed the whole department behind me."

He stepped into the elevator, followed by the two men. He continued standing when the elevator door opened, putting off the confrontation a little longer, and despising himself for it. Finally he pushed himself away from the wall with a thrust of his elbow and strode down the hall. He hesitated at the open door, standing there so long the secretary looked questioningly at him.

"Sheriff, did you need something? The boss is gone for the day. You just missed him."

"Where is he?" Charles wanted to get it over with as quickly as possible. "I need to talk to him now."

"Well, he called someone, introduced himself, and told this person to gas it up and do the check. I'm not sure what he was talking about."

"I am," Charles said grimly. He turned and walked into the office, closing the door behind him. Raul and Meenie were looking at an object tucked inside a long survey-map case. "Did you find it?"

Meenie scratched his bald spot, then replaced his hat. "Yeah, but it wasn't in this thing when we searched it the other night. I wonder where the hell he hid it?"

Raul upended the tube, letting the twenty-two rifle fall onto the desk. He leaned over and sniffed at the barrel. Taking a pen, he hooked it through the trigger guard and turned the gun over. A long scratch marred the gleaming walnut stock. The three men studied it carefully, Raul shaking his head in puzzlement. A muttered exclamation from Meenie drew Charles's and Raul's attention to the edge of the rifle stock where it fit against the barrel. There, caught between the barrel and the stock, was a tiny gray-green frond. The three men turned to the window. Outside, a massive spruce tree grew so close to the building it brushed the glass.

"The old shell game," Meenie said with disgust. "He hid it in the tree until we finished searching inside. Then he just dropped it in this map tube. The only mistake he made in this whole thing was not being a better shot."

"He made another mistake, Meenie," Charles said. "He killed someone in the first place." The shock was wearing off, being replaced by a growing anger and grief. He stared at the rifle lying on the desk, a silent, innocent object, except when used by man. "Take it upstairs and tag it," Charles said abruptly. "I'm going to the airport. I hope to hell it's not too late."

"Raul, you do the honors," Meenie said over his shoulder as he followed Charles out the door.

"Why me?" Raul objected.

"Because you and the sheriff are just a little too decent. Now me, I don't hardly trust anybody. I figure the sheriff might need somebody like that."

Meenie hurried to catch up with Charles, unsnapping his holster as he went. The sheriff might think that damn killer would allow himself to be led back like a bull with a ring through its nose, but Meenie didn't think so. No man who did what that one did was going to come peaceable. If there was any shooting to be done, Meenie was going to do it. The sheriff had enough on his plate just facing facts.

Meenie climbed into the car beside Charles. "What do you think you're doing?" Charles demanded. "I told you to tag that rifle. I don't need any help. I told you he won't hurt me."

"Raul can tag that rifle; it don't take two of us. I'm going with you. Besides, you're wasting time arguing with me. Are we going to the airport or not?"

"We'll talk about this later," Charles said as he switched on the flashing lights. He concentrated on his driving, using the siren only until they were outside Carroll. He ignored the speedometer as it hovered near the hundred-miles-an-hour mark. The fields on either side were a green blur, the wind noise from the high speed making conversation difficult. Charles applied the brakes viciously, causing his body to pull against his safety harness. The car fishtailed into the airport, coming to a screaming stop in front of the hangars. A red-and-white single-engine plane was parked at the edge of the runway, two men standing by the cockpit. Charles unfastened his safety harness and jumped from the car to run toward the plane.

"L.D.!" Charles shouted. "You're not going anywhere."

# CHAPTER

# 20

L.D. HESITATED A MOMENT, HIS EYES SHIFTING FROM Charles to Meenie and back again. He stepped closer to the open cockpit door and rested one hand on the frame. His face was relaxed, a welcoming smile stretching his mouth to reveal even white teeth. "Charles!" he exclaimed. "What are you doing here?"

Charles's stern features mirrored not only his reluctance to accuse his friend but also his doubt. There could be an explanation for all the damning evidence. But even as he thought that, Charles knew he was wrong. There were no explanations. L.D. had killed two people, and attempted to kill two more.

He stopped a few feet from his friend, his eyes focused on the boyishly handsome face of the shorter man. "You know why I'm here, don't you?"

"No, I can't imagine," L.D. replied easily. "I was getting ready to do a little flying, running away from the office for an afternoon. I didn't tell my secretary where I was going. How did you find me?" he asked curiously.

"Your secretary overheard you telling someone to gas up your plane," Charles said. "I've got to take you in, L.D."

L.D. shifted his body to lean back against the open cockpit. "What do you mean, you've got to take me in? What are you talking about, Charles?"

"I'm arresting you for the murder of Maria Martinez and Billy Joe Williams," Charles stated. A startled cry from the other man caused him to snap his head around. He heard Meenie's profane expression at the same time the second man's identity registered on his brain.

"Roberto!" Charles gasped, "What are you doing here?"

Roberto didn't answer. Instead, his face twisting with grief and hate, he hurled himself at L.D. The shot threw him backward to sprawl limply on the asphalt.

Charles stopped in midturn when L.D.'s voice snapped a command. "Don't move! I didn't kill him. If either of you cause me any problems, I will. And don't look around for the airport manager or that kid; they're at Frontier Days. The two of you and Roberto are the only ones to bid me bon voyage. Now turn around, and carefully, very carefully, drop your guns on the ground." L.D. stood calmly by the plane, no longer a relaxed figure but an alert one, his hand curved firmly around a revolver.

He waited patiently while Charles and Meenie disarmed themselves. "Now put your hands on top of your heads, and walk toward the hangars. I'll tell you when to stop."

Charles heard Meenie cursing helplessly as they started walking. "I'm sorry, Meenie. You were right. He won't hesitate to kill anyone to get away. I should have treated him as I would have any other killer," Charles said in a low voice.

"No talking, Charles," L.D. commanded. "Now turn around."

L.D. stood with the discarded guns tucked in his waistband. "You may have some difficulty explaining to the county commission how you both lost your guns. I'll tell you what I'll do. I'll try to throw them out the window after I'm airborne." L.D. began backing toward the waiting plane, his eyes never shifting from Charles and Meenie.

"Why did you do it, L.D.?" Charles cried, his need to know overriding his caution. "Just tell me why," he pleaded, bringing his hands down to spread them in an eloquent gesture.

L.D.'s face twisted with fury. "That damn dumb Mexican bitch wanted me to marry her. Can you believe that? She expected me to divorce Angie to marry her. I tried to reason with her; I told her I would pay for an abortion, then help her with school expenses. It would have been a cheap way out. But no, she didn't believe in abortions. She was going to tell Angie, break up my marriage. My career would never have recovered from the scandal."

Charles felt sick. "Why did you do it to Angie? Even if nothing had happened, why did you cheat on Angie?"

L.D.'s lip curled in derision. "Have you always been in love with my wife, Charles?" He laughed at the guilty flush that darkened Charles skin. "Oh, I knew. But I could trust you. You're too noble to take what you want if it belongs to another man. I used to watch you with her. You looked like a lovesick kid trailing around after her. How does it feel to commit adultery in your heart? I'm sure it's not nearly as satisfying as committing it in reality."

"Didn't you love Angie?" Anger was beginning to overcome Charles.

"Angie was a good wife, Charles. We were childhood sweethearts, you know. But she was perfectly satisfied to live in the old hometown. She had no ambition to be someone, and she was unhappy about my political plans. Sometimes she bored me. The world doesn't begin and end in Carroll, Texas. I wanted to get out—to find some excitement, some challenge. That's why I liked you: you were from the outside world. But you were turning into just another Crawford County aficionado, satisfied with its boundaries. I began to hate you because you had thrown away the kind of life I wanted."

"You're telling me you had an affair because you were bored?" Charles asked in disbelief.

L.D. looked amused. "You don't think that is an adequate reason? Surely you can't believe I was in love with Maria." L.D. laughed with genuine good humor. "You can't believe a man can have an affair because he's bored, because he feels life is passing him by? You didn't grow up in Crawford County. You weren't forced from birth to conform to its stupid standards until you felt rebellion boiling inside you. I wasn't content with life on Crawford County's terms."

"There's nothing wrong with the county's standards; in fact, they're commendable. There's still a strong moral code and the majority try to abide by it. It's a good place to live, L.D. You're what's wrong, not the county."

L.D. uttered an expletive. "Don't tell me about Carroll, Charles; I've lived here all my life. I can name every hypocrite in town."

"I can name a few myself, L.D. But you can't expect the town to take the blame for your crimes. You aren't poor; no one has cheated you, or pushed you around. On the contrary, you have everything a man could want. Some sickness prevents you from being content. I'm only surprised you managed to hide it so well. I didn't have a clue as to how unfeeling you were until you said Maria and Billy Joe weren't worth an ulcer."

"I thought I covered that little slip very well, Charles."

"Oh, you did, but only because you were my friend. If I had been objective, I would have known only a man capable of murder could make a statement like that. But you were depending on the fact I wouldn't be suspicious of my friend. You must have been amused to see me running around in circles trying to find suspects to fit my criteria."

"It was rather handy to have a direct line into the investigation. And I knew I could count on you to turn a blind eye toward any of my out-of-character remarks."

"The remarks weren't out of character, I just wasn't aware of how they reflected your real thinking."

"I meant to tell you, Charles, how much I appreciated your allowing me to sit in the patrol car the morning Maria's body was uncovered. I was a little concerned about making a statement. I wasn't sure you wouldn't check it. Or rather, what really worried me was that you would send out that bowlegged cowboy. You never take anybody at face value, do you Meenie?"

"Nope, and I sure should have gotten out of that car with my gun drawn." Meenie shifted his tobacco and spat on the asphalt.

"Shut up, Meenie!" L.D. screamed. "I don't have to listen to some two-bit county deputy. You're just a nobody!"

"At least I can look in the mirror in the morning and not see a lyin' murderer," Meenie sneered, disgust evident in every line of his body.

"Don't make me mad," L.D. panted, raising his gun to aim it at the middle of Meenie's chest.

"For God's sake, shut up, Meenie!" Charles desperately wanted to gag his deputy.

"That's right, Meenie, do what the sheriff tells you. He's a little bit smarter. Tell me, Charles, before I seek a new identity somewhere else, just what did Old Ben tell you? I presume it was something he told you that finally allowed you to put the pieces together in the right way."

"He saw your pickup and remembered part of the license tag," Charles said dully.

"I killed his dog, you know," L.D. said in a conversational tone of voice. "I didn't know it was his until he got himself locked up. Then I made the connection. I didn't know if he could identify me or not, but I couldn't take the chance. When I talked to him in jail, he was scared to death. I knew then I had to kill him. But you wouldn't cooperate, Charles; you were planning to keep him in jail. I thought I was persuasive that day, don't you agree?"

"Yes, you were. I should have wondered why you were so anxious for me to release him, but I just didn't suspect you. I had all the facts, I just didn't interpret them correctly."

"Oh, well, we can't all be perfect. I nearly made a mistake with Miss Poole, though. You've no idea how shocked I was to find out she didn't know a thing. The stupid old woman should have kept her mouth shut. If I hadn't had to shoot her, it might have been an hour or more before Juan thought to check Old Ben. It was a narrow escape for me. I thought someone had seen me run down the hall to my office. Once inside, it was merely a matter of hiding the gun in the tree and going out the window. I must admit I was a little shaken by the second search. I just had a couple of minutes to put the gun back in the tree before your heavy-handed deputies were tearing through my files. If I had been five minutes later, I would have been making this little speech then instead of today."

"For God's sake, L.D., don't you feel any remorse at all? Didn't you know Maria was still alive when you buried her?" Charles was desperate to know that somewhere in the soul of the man was regret.

For a split second L.D. paled and the hand holding the gun trembled. "Of course I didn't know that she was still alive. I would never have let her die like that if I had known. And I do feel remorse. I didn't want to kill anyone, not even Maria. But she wouldn't listen to reason. And then things got out of hand. I had to keep killing, to protect myself. But at least none of my victims were particularly productive citizens.''

Charles felt both moral outrage and sorrow. There was nothing left of the L.D. he knew. "What about Angie? She's not a nonproductive citizen, she's your wife, for God's sake. You're leaving her and your children to face the town. Can you imagine what it's going to be like for them? Don't you at least care about your children? Someone will always be reminding them their father was a murderer.''

For a moment L.D.'s eyes revealed his anguish. "I know what you mean, Charles. But I'm not worried. Angie can always move somewhere else and change her name." His face cleared as though a bothersome problem had been solved. "Yes, that's what she can do. Take care of it, will you?''

"Angie grew up here, L.D., her family is here. How could you destroy her?''

"Oh, for God's sake, Charles, don't be so melodramatic. I'm not destroying her. She can move back to the ranch with her father. By the time the kids start school, everyone will have forgotten about Maria and Billy Joe." There was a desperate tone to L.D.'s voice, as if some forsaken human quality were trying to surface.

"You're mad, L.D." Charles said; "completely insane.''

"Shut up, Charles, before you make me angry. You think I'm mad because you're obsolete, an anachronism. I'm just looking out for myself. Unfortunately, things didn't work out quite like I planned, but I'm an optimist. I'll do all right for myself. Now, if you and Meenie will just step into that hangar behind you, I'll lock the door. I'm sure you can break out, but it'll take a while. I'll throw your guns out. It's the least I can do when you two have been so cooperative.''

Charles and Meenie looked at one another. Meenie shrugged his shoulders. "I don't see nothin' else we can do, Sheriff. He's got the gun, and I don't figure on arguing.''

"Well, well, Meenie, you are intelligent after all. I suggest you take his advice, Charles. It might be a little hot in there, but at least you'll be alive to feel it. I do want you to know the only reason I don't shoot you is because I was fond of you at one time. In spite of what you think, I don't kill unnecessarily.''

Charles gestured toward Roberto. "L.D., let me bring him inside, too, or at least let me do some emergency first aid. You might not have killed him, but he's going to bleed to death if I don't help him."

L.D. walked over to Roberto's still form and studied it. "He's not bleeding too badly, Charles. I just shot him through the shoulder. I think he'll live. Maybe he'll even unlock the door for you—that is, if he regains consciousness and can figure out how," L.D. motioned with his gun. "Now into the hangar, and back into the far corner."

Charles and Meenie walked into the hot, still air of the hangar. Charles's eyes swept the floor and walls, searching for some means to jimmy the door. The hangar was completely empty, and his shoulders slumped in defeat. He had been beaten at every turn. He swung around as he heard L.D. grasp the door to pull it shut. "Why the hell don't you just shoot yourself and save your family some misery?"

"Now why ever should I do that? My family will survive. Suicide! That's almost humorous, Charles, but just the kind of thing you would do. Goodbye, old friend. I did enjoy your friendship for a while. If it makes you feel any better, I wish I had not been forced into killing Maria. In many ways, she was quite satisfactory. I won't be seeing you again, so take care of Angie, will you. I'm sure that's a job you'll relish." L.D.'s mocking laughter seemed to hang in the air long after the door was closed.

Charles looked at Meenie, knowing the words had to be said. "Meenie," he began hesitantly.

Meenie spat into the corner, then met Charles's eyes. "Hell, Sheriff, I knew how you felt about Mrs. Lassiter, and I don't think any less of you for it. You ain't the kind to go around sleeping with someone else's wife. I ain't about to tell anyone what that bastard said about you and his wife. She's gonna need you bad, and I ain't gonna have her feelin' uneasy around you. I ain't gonna say any more about it; I've already forgot."

Charles clasped his hand on Meenie's shoulder, and nodded.

"Thanks. Now let's see what we can do about getting ourselves out of this mess."

Inserting his fingers in the crack between the door and its frame, he attempted to pull it open. Finally he stopped to slump on the hangar floor. "I can't exert enough pressure. I think we might be able to pull out the steel hook the padlock is fastened to, if we had something to use as a lever."

Meenie looked at the hangar door, crawling along the floor to examine its full length. He spat on the asphalt, and hunkered down on the floor. "You know, Sheriff, no offense, but you ain't very good at tearing things up or making do. Take this door, for instance. You want to lever off the padlock. That doesn't damage the door too bad. Now me, I figure we can kick hell out of this corregated tin at the bottom. It's just nailed on the wooden frame. It shouldn't take too long to kick the nails out, and bend the tin back enough to get out."

"I knew your head was useful for something besides holding your hat. Let's start pushing, not kicking. I haven't heard L.D. start his engines yet. I don't want him to come over here and shoot us if he thinks we have a good chance of getting out quickly."

Charles sat down and leaned against the door. Digging his heels into the floor of the hangar, he pushed against the tin with his shoulders. He felt the rippled metal dig into his back and clenched his teeth together. He kept up a steady pressure and felt it give a little. The sound of the plane engine was startlingly loud in the hangar.

"I reckon we can kick now, Sheriff. He ain't goin' to hear us over that engine."

"Why hasn't he taken off yet?" Charles asked, yelling over the sound of the engines and the dull banging of their boots against the door.

"I don't know. Maybe he's still checking the plane. He's careful, I'll give him that. If Old Ben hadn't been around, L.D. would be sittin' in the legislature next year."

Charles got up and put his eye to the narrow crack in the door. "He's climbing in the cockpit now. Which way is the wind blowing?"

"From the north, I think. Hell, it blows so much I don't

rightly keep up with which direction it's comin' from. What does that have to do with anything?''

"He has to take off into the wind. That means he'll have to taxi to the end of the runway and turn around. If one of us can get out of here and get to the car, we might be able to block the runway and prevent his takeoff.''

Charles sat down on the floor and braced his arms behind him. He bent his legs under his chin and let loose with a powerful kick. Out of the corner of his eye, he saw Meenie get up. "What are you doing?''

"There's someone outside this hangar that could help us. Hey, Roberto!'' Meenie shouted. "Come here, son. We need you.''

"What are you yelling for? He's unconscious.''

Meenie shook his head. "I was watching him while you were jawing with L.D. He's not unconscious, he's just pretending to be. Pretty smart, I'd say. Old L.D. was just looking for an excuse to kill someone. Roberto didn't want to be the one. See, here he comes. Roberto, hurry it up!''

Charles peered through the crack to see Roberto stumble toward the hangar. "My God, I thought he was dying.''

"He's a tough kid, Sheriff. He was a Green Beret in Vietnam. He would've killed L.D. if he could have gotten his hands on him.''

"Sheriff, what can I do?'' Roberto's voice was weak, and he swayed against the hangar door.

"Hey, son, hang in there just a little longer. There's a riot gun in the patrol car. Get it and blow this lock off,'' Meenie said before Charles had a chance to interrupt.

"He doesn't need to shoot the lock off, Meenie. He can pry if off with a hammer; there's one in the tool box in the trunk.''

"Yep,'' Meenie said.

Charles turned white at the thought of what Meenie had just done. He kicked the door in a frenzy, then sat down again.

He heard the echoing of the riot gun over the sound of L.D.'s plane. Hearing the cough of the plane's engine, he clambered to his feet and put his eye to the crack in the door.

He saw Roberto resting the riot gun on the hood of the car, its butt pressing against his uninjured shoulder. He saw him jerk back from the recoil as he fired again. The sheet of flame blocked out the sun as the plane exploded. "No!" Charles screamed.

Meenie grasped his arm. "It's all over, Sheriff," he said. "Here, sit down and stay still. If you need to throw up, go ahead and do it. I ain't goin' to think anything about it. He was your friend, and a man ought to feel something for his friends."

Charles breathed shallowly through his mouth to control his nausea. "He wasn't my friend. The L.D. I knew wasn't the man who died in that plane. I didn't think I was so bad a judge of character I could've been fooled for three years."

"I don't know, Sheriff," Meenie said. "I think L.D. was crazier than a horse that's been eatin' loco weed. I just didn't know him well enough to say how long he's been that way. I think he was the kind of crazy that hides real well."

Meenie turned back and put his eye to the crack. "Hey, you hear that? It sounds like a siren. I think old Raul finally got the gun tagged. Sure as hell took him long enough."

Charles walked out of the hangar, carefully putting one foot in front of the other. Not even Vietnam had left him feeling so sick. He saw Roberto leaning against the wheel of the car, fresh blood running down his arm to soak into the asphalt.

"Are you satisfied, Roberto, that Maria has been avenged?"

Roberto leaned his head back against the side of the car, his eyes feverish with pain and something else, a sorrow too deep for expression. "I'm satisfied, Sheriff, but I am not happy. Death does not make a man happy."

Charles nodded his head and continued to walk, a decision made. He focused his eyes on the oily column of smoke rising from the wrecked plane. Unaware of the tears that streaked his face, he silently bade farewell to his friend.

# EPILOGUE

CHARLES LEANED BACK IN HIS CHAIR, HIS FEET propped up on his desk, and watched the wind whip the yellow-brown leaves off the giant elm trees outside his windows. The trees were almost bare, and Halloween was still two weeks away. The old timers said it meant an early winter. Charles couldn't support or deny their claim; this was only his fourth fall season in the Texas Panhandle. He heard the low murmur of voices from the outer office that meant the day shift was coming on duty.

He laced his fingers together behind his head and wondered why he came to work so early; there was very little to do that couldn't wait until eight o'clock. But there was nowhere else to go. He could hardly stop by Angie's for coffee at seven o'clock in the morning as he had done when L.D. was alive. Quickly his mind sought a distraction; he still avoided thinking of L.D. When Meenie stuck his head around the corner of the door, Charles greeted him eagerly.

"Meenie, you grizzled old cowboy reject, come tell me about your trip."

Meenie sank into the chair closest to the spitoon. "You're makin' it sound like a vacation—just a tour around beautiful Huntsville with a side trip to the state prison. Hell, you shoulda been stuck in a car for two days with Sammy. You know what the warden said when I got to the prison? He took one look at Sammy and said he wished you'd send a little higher class of criminal next time. He said Sammy just wasn't up to the standards of his establishment."

"What did you tell him?" Charles asked, enjoying himself for the first time since confronting L.D.

"I told him Crawford County was testing his new rehabilitation program."

Charles leaned his head back and laughed. "If the warden can rehabilitate Sammy, he can try walking on water next. When did you get back?"

"About one o'clock this morning," Meenie replied. "Wasn't any reason to hang around, so I came on back. How's everything around here?"

"You've only been gone four days, Meenie. What did you expect to happen?"

Meenie eyed Charles critically. "I called Raul after I got home. He said you were still in one piece, but the cracks were beginning to show."

Charles felt an instant irritability. "That doesn't sound like Raul."

"He didn't say it like that. You know Raul; he talks a whole lot better than I do. I figure it's because he's still tryin' to prove he ain't a wetback. But anyway, you know what he meant. You still feeling guilty, Sheriff? You tryin' to work twice as hard to make up for lyin'?"

Charles pulled his feet off the desk and sat up straight, inwardly flinching as Meenie's words stripped away his defenses, forcing him to come to terms with himself. "I had to protect Angie; that was my first thought. I didn't seem to care about anything else. If I had charged Roberto with L.D.'s murder, the whole dirty mess would have been dragged through the court. Angie's life would have been ruined, and Maria's family humiliated. L.D. died as a result of the violence he initiated. As Miss Poole said, sometimes there is poetic justice."

Charles was silent for a moment, consciously sorting through his feelings for the first time. "You set me up, didn't you, Meenie?"

Meenie shifted uncomfortably on his chair. "I guess I did kind of set you up. I didn't think of it that way at the time. I better quit, Sheriff; you can't trust me, I guess, and I don't think you can work with someone you don't trust. But if I had it to do all over again, I'd act the same way."

"No, Meenie, I don't want you to quit. I still had a choice.

I didn't have to make the decision I did. But the innocent have been protected. Angie can grieve for the image of her husband, instead of knowing the reality. L.D.'s children can grow up with stories of their father as he should have been, rather than what he was. And, damn it, I think that's all right.''

Charles walked to the window and watched the wind scattering the fallen leaves, covering the sidewalk with a crisp yellow gold carpet. He turned back to Meenie, bracing his hands on the windowsill behind him. ''I guess I'll always feel a little guilty. After all, I did take an oath to uphold the laws of this state. Somewhere down the line I'll have to pay the price for breaking those laws. But if I had to live that day again—if all of us did: you, me, Raul, Roberto—I believe we would bind ourselves together with the same lie. L.D. died in a freak plane crash, Roberto shot himself cleaning a gun, and the murders were committed by a person or persons unknown. That is a truth everyone can live with.''

''Everybody but you,'' Meenie said softly. ''Lyin', even for a good cause, just don't set well with you.''

''That's between me and my conscience. I'll learn to live with it. But enough of the past. How about calling Raul in here, and let's try my new dispatcher's coffee.''

Meenie shifted his tobacco and spat into the spitoon. ''It can't be any worse than Slim's coffee. Who's the new dispatcher, and how did you get rid of Mabel?''

''I merely transferred her to the midnight shift so I personally wouldn't have to see the woman except during emergencies.''

Charles strolled over to his phone and buzzed the outer office. ''Tell Raul to come in, and bring us some coffee, please.'' Charles hung up and slid into his chair, a complacent look on his face.

Raul opened the door and let a spritely old lady carrying a tray laden with three cups and saucers, cream and sugar, precede him into the office.

''Good morning, Sheriff, Meenie. I hope you like the coffee,'' Miss Poole said briskly. ''In spite of its recent bad press, I have always been of the opinion a good cup of coffee is the only civilized way to start the day.''

Miss Poole put the tray on the corner of Charles's desk and poured steaming hot coffee from a thermos pitcher. The three men pulled their chairs closer and accepted the cups from her, a gleam of anticipation in their eyes.

Charles took the first sip, and immediately called upon a lifetime of self-control. Carefully setting his cup back on its saucer, he cleared his throat. "Your coffee certainly has character, Miss Poole."

Miss Poole beamed, if such a prim, dignified lady could be said to beam. "Thank you, Sheriff. I believe a man needs strong coffee. That liquid Slim made the other day doesn't deserve the name." Miss Poole opened the door and called over her shoulder. "Call me when you're ready for another pot."

The three men looked at the closed door, then at their coffee. Raul was the first to break the silence. "When I was a little kid, I chewed on a piece of tar. I remember it tasted just like that coffee."

Charles raised his cup to propose a toast. "Here's to Miss Poole. If she actually enjoys coffee like this, she's a better man than any of us."